Knowing Your Worth

Billionaire Banker Series, Volume 4

Lexy Timms

Published by Dark Shadow Publishing, 2018.

This is a work of fiction. Similarities to real people, places, or events are entirely coincidental.

KNOWING YOUR WORTH

First edition. October 29, 2018.

Copyright © 2018 Lexy Timms.

Written by Lexy Timms.

Also by Lexy Timms

Billionaire Banker Series
Banking on Him
Price of Passion
Investing in Love
Knowing Your Worth

Billionaire Holiday Romance Series
Driving Home for Christmas
The Valentine Getaway
Cruising Love

Billionaire in Disguise Series
Facade
Illusion
Charade

Billionaire Secrets Series
The Secret
Freedom
Courage
Trust
Impulse
Billionaire Secrets Box Set Books #1-3

Building Billions
Building Billions - Part 1
Building Billions - Part 2
Building Billions - Part 3

Conquering Warrior Series
Ruthless

Diamond in the Rough Anthology
Billionaire Rock
Billionaire Rock - part 2

Dominating PA Series
Her Personal Assistant - Part 1
Her Personal Assistant Box Set

Fake Billionaire Series
Faking It
Temporary CEO
Caught in the Act
Never Tell A Lie
Fake Christmas

One That Came Back
One You Never Leave
One Christmas Night
Hades' Spawn MC Complete Series

Hard Rocked Series
Rhyme
Harmony
Lyrics

Heart of Stone Series
The Protector
The Guardian
The Warrior

Heart of the Battle Series
Celtic Viking
Celtic Rune
Celtic Mann
Heart of the Battle Series Box Set

Heistdom Series
Master Thief
Goldmine
Diamond Heist
Smile For Me

Senior Advisor to the Boss
Forever the Boss
Christmas With the Boss
Billionaire in Control
Gift for the Boss - Novella 3.5
Managing the Bosses Box Set #1-3

Model Mayhem Series
Shameless
Modesty
Imperfection

Moment in Time
Highlander's Bride
Victorian Bride
Modern Day Bride
A Royal Bride
Forever the Bride

Outside the Octagon
Submit

Protecting Diana Series
Her Bodyguard
Her Defender
Her Champion

Her Protector

Her Forever

Protecting Layla Series

His Mission

His Objective

His Devotion

Racing Hearts Series

Rush

Pace

Fast

Reverse Harem Series

Primals

Archaic

Unitary

RIP Series

Track the Ripper

Hunt the Ripper

Pursue the Ripper

R&S Rich and Single Series

Alex Reid
Parker

Saving Forever
Saving Forever - Part 1
Saving Forever - Part 2
Saving Forever - Part 3
Saving Forever - Part 4
Saving Forever - Part 5
Saving Forever - Part 6
Saving Forever Part 7
Saving Forever - Part 8
Saving Forever Boxset Books #1-3

Shifting Desires Series
Jungle Heat
Jungle Fever
Jungle Blaze

Southern Romance Series
Little Love Affair
Siege of the Heart
Freedom Forever
Soldier's Fortune

Tattooist Series

Confession of a Tattooist
Surrender of a Tattooist
Heart of a Tattooist
Hopes & Dreams of a Tattooist

Tennessee Romance
Whisky Lullaby
Whisky Melody
Whisky Harmony

The Bad Boy Alpha Club
Battle Lines - Part 1
Battle Lines

The Brush Of Love Series
Every Night
Every Day
Every Time
Every Way
Every Touch

The Debt
The Debt: Part 1 - Damn Horse
The Debt: Complete Collection

Love & College
Billionaire Heart
First Love
Frisky and Fun Romance Box Collection
Beating Hades' Bikers

Watch for more at www.lexytimms.com.

Knowing
Your Worth

By Lexy Timms

Copyright 2018

All rights reserved.
Knowing Your Worth
Billionaire Banker Series #4
Copyright 2018 by Lexy Timms
Cover by: Book Cover by Design[1]

---

1. http://bookcoverbydesign.co.uk/

Billionaire Banker Series

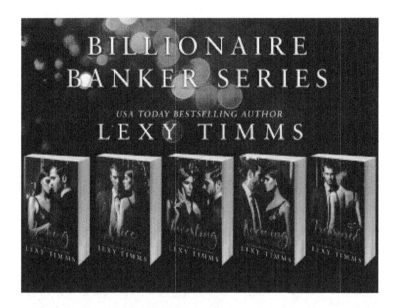

Book 1 – Banking on Him
Book 2 – Price of Passion
Book 3 – Investing in Love
Book 4 – Knowing Your Worth
Book 5 – Treasured Forever

Find Lexy Timms:

LEXY TIMMS NEWSLETTER:
  http://eepurl.com/9i0vD
  Lexy Timms Facebook Page:
  https://www.facebook.com/SavingForever
  Lexy Timms Website:
  http://www.lexytimms.com

Want to read more...
For **FREE**?
Sign up for Lexy Timms' newsletter
And she'll send you updates on new releases, ARC copies of books
and a whole lotta fun!
Sign up for news and updates!
http://eepurl.com/9i0vD

Knowing Your Worth Blurb

BY USA TODAY BESTSELLING Author, Lexy Timms.

Love like you're never counting the cost.

Bethany Walker wakes up in the hospital with a head injury and no memory of her attacker or how she got there. Worse, she learns her father is back in jail and her family is headed for a crisis.

Now an even bigger threat looms as an unseen enemy stalk her from the shadows, ready to take her down with her father. The only person she can lean on is her boyfriend, Kirk Sterling, the man her family blames for all their problems.

After billionaire Kirk Sterling finds an unconscious Bethany, he vows to make his enemies pay for going after her.

With his powerful parents now locked up in jail and his financial empire crumbling around him, fighting back won't be easy. A new danger threatens to destroy everything he holds dear, including Bethany.

Will their relationship be enough to help them survive, or will they pay with their lives?

Chapter 1

The ambulance sirens blared so loudly they almost drowned out his panicked thoughts. Two EMTs were speedily helping Bethany, who lay motionless on a stretcher.

Kirk sat crammed in one of the seats, watching desperately for signs of life. He reached his hand out to her.

One of the EMTs frowned and shook his head. "No. Sir, you're going to have to let us do our job, okay?"

The EMT's voice sounded muffled as Kirk's thoughts turned to an incessant roar. Kirk didn't know what he said in response. He was too focused on Bethany to notice anything.

She lay on the stretcher, eyes shut, skin as pale as chalk. This wasn't the peace of sleep. He'd often wake to find her sleeping after they'd made love. When she slept, her body was always warm. Her cheeks always rosy. Now she looked... lifeless.

Seeing her like this broke his heart into pieces. Pieces so fine they might as well have been dust.

"Sir? Can you hear me?" The EMT gently shook his shoulder, pulling him from his agonized thoughts. "Did you see the object that was used to hit her?"

"No," Kirk said, his voice gruff with emotion. Whoever had ransacked her apartment had hit her. Hit her hard enough for him to wonder if she was even still alive. "I didn't see."

"And you say you found her like this?" the EMT pressed.

Surprised at his tone, Kirk's gaze jerked up to the EMT. Did they think he had something to do with this? Anger made him clench his teeth. "I found her. Tried to revive her, but it didn't work. That's when I called 911."

The EMT nodded. "Got it. I understand that this is difficult sir, but we have to ask these questions. It's our job."

Their job. That brought Kirk out of his haze of anger and back to reality. The EMTs were trying to save her. They'd even been good enough to let Kirk into the ambulance. Probably a breach in protocol. Right now he couldn't afford to give in to despair. He had to shove his shock aside and be there for her. Even though he had no medical expertise, he'd channel his strength to her. Surely that might help to bring her back.

While the EMTs monitored her vital signs Kirk kept his gaze on her, never allowing it to leave her for even a moment.

After sitting in the ambulance for what felt like years, they came to a screeching halt. The EMTs sprang into action, opening the doors and wheeling the stretcher out. They dashed towards the accident and emergency entrance of the hospital, Kirk racing right on their heels.

Inside was a buzz of activity. Medical staff rushed gurneys through double doors. Some of the bloodied patients thrashed around in panic.

"Sir, you need to wait out in the waiting room!" the EMT by Bethany's side shouted.

Kirk sped up, refusing to slow down. "I have to be with her."

"You can't come with her, sir. You aren't family."

That stopped him dead in his tracks as the EMTs rushed through some double doors and disappeared. Bethany's family had to be notified. He shut his eyes, trying to slow down the thoughts that bombarded him.

Her father had been arrested hours ago. Notifying him now would be tricky, if not impossible. That left her mother and her brother, neither of whom were reliable according to the way Bethany had described them. Her mother was an alcoholic and her brother was a wastrel. Now he had to contact them.

As the agony set in, he moved away and walked into the chaotic waiting room. Nurses were talking to frantic relatives; other people in the waiting room looked around, bewildered. A terrible sense of doom washed over him as he searched for an empty seat. When he found one, he stumbled into a chair and pulled out his cell phone.

Kirk dreaded making this call. If Bethany's mom and brother had gotten the news about Lloyd's arrest, news that Bethany had been savagely attacked was only going to add to their pain. He looked through his phone contacts and realized that he only had her brother Joshua's number. With no other options, Kirk made the call. It rang several times and then went to voicemail.

He cringed, indecisive for a split second. Leaving a message would crush her brother, but neglecting to tell him was unfair. Joshua deserved to know that his sister was in serious trouble. Taking a deep breath Kirk left a quick message, stating that Bethany had been hurt and had been taken to the San Diego Medical Hospital. Hopefully the message gave enough detail without causing unnecessary pain.

Now that he'd called the one family member he could reach, there was nothing to be done. He couldn't contact his parents since they had been arrested, too. The waiting room began to tilt. The stress of the situation was getting to him. There was no way he could handle this alone without cracking under the pressure. He needed someone, but couldn't even rely on his own parents. Plus, his brother lived all the way in New York.

Finally, it hit him. Ian. His cousin hadn't been around as much now that he was a newlywed, but Kirk had always been close with him. Once he called his cousin and gave him directions to the hospital, Kirk waited.

An hour later, Ian appeared in the waiting room.

He approached Kirk, concern etched on his face. His suit was rumpled like he'd been through stress of his own. "Damn, Kirk, you look terrible. What happened to Bethany? I didn't even know you guys were still together after—"

Kirk shook his head, cutting him off. "I can't talk in here." The noise in the waiting room was so loud he could barely hear himself think.

"There's a café in the hospital," Ian said. "We'll talk there."

He followed his cousin to the café and grabbed a corner table while Ian got them some coffee.

"Thank you for coming," Kirk said when his cousin came back with two steaming cups.

Ian sat down across from him. "Of course I'd come. There's nothing I wouldn't do for you, Cousin."

"I'm amazed you showed up, considering our family history with the Livingstons."

Ian scratched the stubble on his jaw thoughtfully. "I figured that after you found out she was a Livingston you'd be done with her. Guess I was wrong."

"I thought that, too, at first." Kirk averted his gaze to glance down at the table. His throat tightened. "Now I can't imagine my life without her."

"Even though I don't know Bethany as well as you do, I know she's an optimist. And I know she wouldn't want you to think the worst." Ian took a sip of coffee. "The doctors are working on her, right?"

"Yeah," Kirk said with a nod. "But I doubt they'll give me more information since I'm not family."

"Speaking of family, I heard about her dad's arrest earlier today." Ian's expression turned grim. "And your parents as well."

"Dammit, my parents. They need me, too." He hated this. Hated being caught between his parents and his girlfriend like this. Two disasters had struck today. It was like he was being ripped in half.

"My dad is taking care of things, so don't worry about your parents for now," Ian said.

"Ian, what if your dad gets mixed up in all this?" Kirk asked, lowering his voice. Even though his uncle didn't work at Sterling Investment

Bank, he owned a successful car dealership. The bank and the car dealership shared business partners, and even had lawyers in common. If the police had come down on his parents, they might come after more family members. "What if the police come after him, too?"

"Don't worry. Margaret and her family are going to help—and they have clout," Ian said, referring to his new wife. "There's no way these charges are going to stick. It's got to be a mistake."

Of the two of them, Ian was always the one who looked on the bright side of things. Kirk was a realist most of the time, while Ian was an idealist. If Ian ever worried, it rarely lasted long.

"I don't think the charges are a mistake," Kirk murmured. "This is deliberate. And I think Bethany's attack is connected to it."

Ian's eyebrows shot up in surprise. "How? Wait... I didn't get the full story about Bethany. Someone tried to rob her?"

"I don't know if that was the motive behind it," Kirk said, "but someone attacked her and hit her in the head. The injury looked..." Life-threatening. The air squeezed out of his lungs. Even thinking those words caused an agony beyond reason. Saying them out loud would kill him.

"Okay, so do you know who attacked her?"

"I have my suspicions." Kirk closed his eyes for second, needing to get his bearings. The shock of seeing Bethany in that state had thrown him off. Usually, when disaster struck he didn't sit in waiting rooms. Didn't give in to despair or accept any kind of helplessness. He'd spent enough time wallowing.

He might not have the medical expertise to save Bethany, but he could catch who had done this to her. Catch them and make them pay dearly for hurting her.

"We need to contact the police, then—"

"No. We can't tell the cops anything," Kirk said harshly. "They're in on this."

"What?"

Kirk gave his cousin a hard stare, signaling how important what he was about to say was. "A cop attacked Bethany. We can't trust the police with this."

"Kirk, your parents are probably being questioned by cops right now," Ian said. "Are you sure a cop did this?"

If it wasn't the cop he had in mind, then one of her father's shady connections might have done it. Either way, Kirk had learned that the police couldn't be trusted. For all he knew, his parents had been framed for something they didn't do. "You've got to stop my parents. They can't tell the cops anything."

"I'll call my dad and try to get him to intervene. If your parents get to talk to their lawyers, they can avoid giving anything away to the police." Ian pulled his phone out of his jacket pocket. "What are you going to do in the meantime?"

Kirk grabbed his cup of coffee. "The most important thing is for me to track down Bethany's family." The hospital staff wasn't going to let him near her since he wasn't family. Which meant there was a good chance that when she woke up, she'd be all alone with no one to comfort her. Her father had disowned her weeks ago. That had led to her relationship with her brother falling apart. Plus, her mother was an alcoholic who had walked in and out of Bethany's life for years. All of that had made Bethany feel alone and abandoned. But the only thing worse than having her dysfunctional family around would be for her to wake up and not have anyone by her side.

"I'll go talk to hospital staff and see if they've been able to contact some of her family," Kirk told his cousin.

"Okay, we can meet up in the waiting room when we're done."

As he walked out of the café, Kirk took out his phone again and called Bethany's brother. Still no answer. He headed to the customer service desk at the front of the accident and emergency department. After several minutes waiting in line, he approached the nurse at the desk.

Quickly, he explained the situation. "Has the hospital had any luck getting in touch with her family?"

The nurse frowned. "Sir, we can't give you that kind of information. It's confidential, and only the patient and her family are privy to that kind of information."

"Please." His body went rigid as he fought the onslaught of raw grief welling up in his chest. "You have to help me out here. I've donated to this hospital. You couldn't have renovated this place last year without me." It was a card he hated playing. In any other situation, throwing his privilege around to cut corners would sicken him. But this was Bethany's life. He didn't care what sacrifices he had to make. The principles he'd have to push aside. For Bethany, he'd break every rule and every law to see her safe.

A frail hand on his arm gave him pause, and he looked down. The woman who had grabbed his arm looked familiar. Like Bethany would look decades from now. If she survived. His heart squeezed so tightly, he thought it might stop beating entirely.

Though the woman's clothes were rumpled and her bottle-blonde hair was a matted mess, there was an elegance in the way she held up her chin. Her eyes—as blue as Bethany's—were glassy. In her other hand she held a cup of coffee, though she reeked of alcohol.

"You're Kirk Sterling?" The woman's words were slurred. Her eyes out of focus, as if she was looking right through him at something far away.

He nodded. "Who are you?" he asked, though he could already guess the answer.

She swayed on her feet, so thin and slender he wondered if a breeze might blow her away. A girlish giggle escaped her throat.

"I'm Elle Livingston," she said, her voice a rasp. "Do you know where Bethany is? I'm her mother."

Before he could answer, she lifted her free hand and dumped the hot coffee all over him.

Chapter 2

She was running down a long, dark corridor. With each step she took the walls around her closed in, inch by inch. There was no end in sight. No light at the end. Just a yawning cavern of never-ending darkness.

Her lungs screamed for air as she ran. Barefoot. She had no shoes on. The only clothing she had on was a flimsy gown. Nothing that could protect her from the walls. Suddenly, up ahead she saw a figure as a dim light filled the corridor. Finally. Someone who might help her escape.

Bethany cried out, desperate to get the figure's attention. As the light grew brighter, she saw that the dark figure was familiar to her. Kirk.

The walls were now so close to her that her arms banged into them as she ran. If she didn't get out soon, she'd be crushed to death. Her legs felt as heavy as lead now, but she forced herself to keep going. All she had to do was get to Kirk, and they would both be free of this place.

Finally, she got to him and he pushed her. Pushed her out of the way as the walls closed in on him. Frantic, she lunged for him, fighting to pull him away. A scream escaped her throat. Too late. The walls crushed him and suddenly her world was plunged into darkness.

Her eyes snapped open, a bright white light nearly blinding her. Everything was a stark, unnatural white. The total opposite of the darkness she'd just woken from. Her heart was racing a million miles a minute. In a panic she thrashed around wildly, trying to get free of this place. But she was too weak to even sit upright.

"Bethany? Bethany, can you hear me?"

It was her mother's voice. But how? She hadn't seen her mother in weeks now. Didn't even know where she was.

Suddenly, the room came into focus and her gaze fell on her mother's face.

"*Mom.*" Her chest tightened with emotion. Seeing her mother here banished her terror. It had been a nightmare. Only a bad dream. Relief reminded her to breathe. Her heartbeat slowed.

"I'm here now, kitten," her mother said from the chair beside her bed. "That bad man can't hurt you anymore."

"Bad man?" Her temples throbbed with a sudden onslaught of pain, and she grimaced. She groaned, "My head is killing me."

"Don't worry, hon. The doctors gave you painkillers right when they noticed you were trying to wake up earlier. The pain will go away any minute now." Her mother made soft, cooing noises as she placed her rough palm on Bethany's cheek.

Bethany looked around, her eyes landing on the IV hooked up to her arm. She was in a pristine hospital room that smelled of some strong chemical. A disinfectant of some kind.

"What's going on?" Bethany demanded. "Why am I here?"

Her mother's eyes widened. "Oh, the doctors said you might have a hard time remembering. The bad man hurt you. He attacked you and knocked you out."

Dizziness made the room start to spin. She shut her eyes, trying to make everything go still. Trying to remember what had happened. "How long have I been in the hospital?"

"Since yesterday afternoon, pudding. And it's almost noon now, so you've been sleeping for twenty-four hours." Her mother smiled brightly, a happy glint in her eye. There was something deceptively childlike when her mother was like this.

Bethany's heart sank. Her mother always looked and behaved this way when she drank too much. Weeks ago her father had told her how happy he was that her mother was sober, but it looked like she was back to her old ways.

The hospital room door opened and a doctor dressed in scrubs stepped in. "Hello, Bethany. I'm Dr. Stavropoulos." He smiled as he picked up the clipboard at the foot of her bed. "It says you were given quite a nasty bump on the head. It's a good thing you were brought in so quickly. You've got to react quickly when it comes to head wounds. Your injuries might have caused more permanent damage if you hadn't come in when you did."

Instinctively, she lifted her hand to touch the part of her forehead that felt sore.

"Best not to touch it," Dr. Stavropoulos cautioned. "We gave you a few stitches to close the wound."

"Is it bad?" her mother asked. "Will my baby be okay?"

"We still have to run an MRI scan—"

"I can't afford that," Bethany said.

"Oh, you don't have to worry about all that," the doctor said gently. "The San Diego Medical Hospital never makes patients pay for our emergency services. Our generous donors have made sure of that."

"Okay. That's good to know," she murmured.

"Now, you've had a severe concussion," Dr. Stavropoulos explained as he approached her. "We think you're on your way to a full recovery, but we still have to run some tests. You'll get an MRI scan, and if things look all right we'll be able to discharge you from the hospital as early as tomorrow afternoon."

"So, if everything looks okay, I'll be free to go?" Bethany asked.

The doctor nodded. "Yes, you will. However, you'll have to come back in a few days so we can remove your stitches. After that you should come back to the hospital for some check-ups for the next several weeks. That will give us the chance to monitor you and make sure you're recovering."

"Doctor..." She paused as she struggled through her foggy mind to come up with the words. "My mom says someone hit me, but I can't remember it. What happened?"

"One of the symptoms is short-term memory loss," Dr. Stavropoulos said. "It's nothing to worry about since you should recover your memories relatively quickly. Though it can help to try to think about the last thing you remember."

She swallowed hard. "I remember... I went to an auction." Bethany saw images of the auction flash in her mind. She had gone to the auction with Kirk. They'd found a way to make a lot of money to help people who needed it. Try as she might to push her mind to remember anything after that, she couldn't. It was all just blank. A vast, empty space of nothing. "I don't remember more than that. I don't remember who hurt me."

He glanced at the clipboard in his hand. "As I said, that's to be expected. I spoke with the police department and explained that you weren't in any condition to answer their questions right now. When you do remember, you'll want to get in touch with them. That way they can find whoever did this to you."

The hair on the back of her neck stood up. Whoever had hurt her was still out there. Free to come back and hurt her again. "What if he comes back to hurt me?"

"You're safe while you're in the hospital," Dr. Stavropoulos assured her. "We have excellent security right outside each of the hospital rooms. You have my promise that nobody will hurt you while you're here. And I'm sure the police will want to keep you safe once you contact them and give them more details. For now, you should get some rest."

"Can my mom stay?" she asked.

He nodded. "Yes. You can see your visitors until five in the evening. A nurse will come in to check on you soon, and you'll be able to get your scan tonight or tomorrow morning."

With that he looked her over, and left the room once he was satisfied.

Her mother reached for her hand. "Don't be scared, kitten. I'm here now. That bad man won't ever hurt you again. I won't let him."

Bethany sighed. "Oh, Mom, what can you do against a man I can't even remember?"

"But I saw him," her mother's raspy voice insisted. "I saw him and made him go away. That awful Kirk Sterling won't ever hurt you again."

She bolted upright, searing pain pressing down on her temples from the sudden movement. "You saw Kirk? Where? When?"

"Don't worry, sweetie," her mother said. "I found him and threw my coffee at him. That made him leave. He'll never hit you again."

"Mom... Kirk didn't hit me," Bethany said sharply. "Why did you attack him like that?"

Her mother frowned. "How do you know he didn't? You don't even remember."

"Because Kirk would never hurt me," she said. "He'd rather die than hurt me, or any woman."

"What are you saying? You make it sound like you're friends with him or something." Her mother tilted her head, confusion creasing her eyebrows.

Bethany's stomach tightened with apprehension. Even though her father and brother had discovered her relationship with Kirk, her mother still didn't know. The truth would look like a betrayal to her. "We're more than friends."

"*No.*" Her mother snatched her hand back and jumped unsteadily to her feet. "No, it's not true. You can't do that. You can't do this to me. To us. Not to your family."

"I'm not trying to hurt you. I swear I'm not. Please try to understand," she said.

"Kirk and his awful, low-class parents put your daddy in prison. In prison, Bethany." Her mother's eyes shimmered with unshed tears.

"He's using you so that he can hurt us again. You can't trust him. You can't!"

But she did trust him. With all her heart. A heart that ached to see him now. "Mom... how did you and Kirk even know I'd be in the hospital?"

"He called your brother and left a message. I dropped by his apartment to pick up some clothes. I heard the message that you were hurt and came to the hospital to find you." Tears rolled down her cheeks. "I was so scared. I thought he was the one who hurt you and put you here."

"Kirk probably rescued me and you chased him away." A terrible thought struck her. What if her mother had gone after Kirk so badly he decided to break up with her again?

"Good. I don't want that tacky family near you," her mom said. "You can't date a boy like that."

"Don't say that," she said, more forcefully than she wanted. She had always known that breaking the news about Kirk to her mom might be difficult, but in her mother's state it was like explaining the truth to a petulant child. A child she had to depend on now that she was in the hospital.

"I can say what I want," her mother said. "He isn't good enough for you. That whole family is new- money trash. Bunch of ingrates. They'd still be dirt-poor if it weren't for me and your father taking pity on them."

"I really don't want to have this conversation right now." She blew out a sharp breath as the throbbing in her head got worse. Arguing with her mother was draining her. Robbing her of the little strength she had.

Her mother frowned and then nodded. "Okay, dear. We'll talk about this later. Right now, you need to rest. I'm here with you now. There's nothing to worry about."

She lay back down on the bed and briefly shut her eyes. The best thing to do right now was focus on regaining her strength. Hopefully, her MRI would come back with no problems and she'd be able to go home soon. But as she thought about going home, the reality of her situation sank in. In her state she was completely dependent on her mother, who could barely take care of herself. Her mother was basically an alcoholic, and depending solely on her might not be the best idea.

"Wait... where's Joshua?" she asked, wondering where her brother was. "You said you heard a message on Joshua's phone. Does Joshua know I'm in the hospital? What about Dad?" Tears stung her eyes as she remembered the way her father had disowned her weeks ago. Maybe in her condition he would reach out to her. Maybe there could be a silver lining, and this tragedy could put her family back together after all these years.

"Oh, honey, you don't know." Her mother chewed her bottom lip.

A wave of panic crashed through her. "Don't know what?" Her heart started to race. "Mom, what is it?"

Her mother averted her gaze and stared down at the floor. "It's your father, sweetie. He's back in jail."

Chapter 3

Back in jail.

For a long moment, her mother's words were incomprehensible to her. Bethany's throat tightened as she struggled to breathe. This couldn't be happening. Not now. Not again.

"What are you talking about?" she finally forced out. "How can Dad be back in jail? Did he violate his parole or something?"

"I don't know," her mother said tightly. "I saw the police taking him away on the news and they didn't give any details. After I saw the news I went straight to your brother's apartment. By then Joshua had already gone to see if he could get your dad out. That's when I heard the message on his phone."

The news was so shocking Bethany could feel herself start to go numb. "Does Joshua know I'm in the hospital?"

Her mother nodded. "Yes, he does. I told him, and he was ready to come down to see you, but I begged him to focus on getting your dad out. So Joshua is doing what he can to find money to bail out your father. That is, if they even agree to grant him bail."

This was worse than her nightmare. Her worst fear come to life. Memories of the day her father had been arrested the first time flashed in her mind. It had been on her seventeenth birthday. The final year of her childhood. She had been looking forward to last year of her carefree, privileged life as an heiress. And then, the police had barged in and dragged her father away. It had been the worst day of her life.

What followed was even worse. For years after, she could only see her father when she visited him in prison. She shuddered at the memory of walking through the huge prison gates. Of walking underneath the barbed wire and stepping into the gloomiest, most terrifying place she had ever seen.

An ache was building in her chest and she gripped the bed sheet tightly for strength. "He'll need a lawyer. Even if he gets bailed out, he's going to need someone to represent him. To fight for him."

"More money." Her mother's shoulders drooped. "That's all there ever is. Something that needs money we don't have anymore."

She thought of the money she and Kirk had taken from Damien Kemp. That money was probably in a foundation now, and she knew in her heart that had been the right thing to do. If she told her mother about it, though, she would never have any peace. As desperate as her family was for money, she had sworn to give it back to the victims of her father's alleged crimes. Those people had suffered enough, and she would never forgive herself for putting them through even more stress by denying them the funds that they needed now.

"We'll figure out a way to raise the funds," Bethany said, with more confidence than she felt. If her father was accused of another major crime, the bail would be astronomically high. And getting a good lawyer was going to be costly. She hoped that this was all just a misunderstanding, or a minor issue with his parole. Otherwise, her father would be in serious trouble all over again. Trouble that could send him away for months or years.

Even though her dad had disowned her, the thought of losing him a second time was almost too much to bear. Her heart squeezed as pain snaked through her.

The hospital room door swung open suddenly and Kirk stepped inside. Though he was immaculately dressed, he looked exhausted. His eyes were bloodshot, and concern was etched on his handsome face. But seeing him now eased some of her agony.

"Kirk. You're here." She scrambled to sit up again.

Her mother's eyes narrowed and she whirled around to look at him. "You can't come in here. Not after what you've done. If you take one more step I'll call the cops."

———◆———

HE DIDN'T KNOW IF SHE was being serious or not. It might have been the threat of a drunk woman. Then again, it might be the threat of a terrified mother just trying to protect her daughter. Either way, Kirk knew he was going to have to take Elle Livingston very seriously.

"I'm not trying to cause trouble." He held up the vase of roses in his hands like a peace offering. "I just want to see Bethany."

Elle balled up her hands and glared at him. "You did this to her. You hurt my baby."

"Mom, he didn't hurt me!" Bethany cried from her bed.

His eyes fell on her and the sight nearly broke his heart all over again. She looked so fragile. Though some of the color had come back to her face, the stitches in her forehead terrified him. She had only been in the hospital for a day, but she was thinner now. With shadows underneath her eyes. And worst of all, she was hooked up to an IV. Seeing her look so diminished and helpless in the huge bed was like a dagger through him.

"I didn't do this, Mrs. Livingston," he said, voice thick with emotion. "I would never hurt your daughter. I swear I could never ever do something like this."

Elle's lip curled in disdain. "What do you want?"

All he wanted to do now was to be with Bethany. Stay by her side until she was well enough to leave the hospital. After Elle had dumped hot coffee on him yesterday, he'd stayed away to give Bethany's mother space. Time to cool off after finding out that her only daughter had been attacked. He had stayed in the waiting room after his hostile encounter with Elle to avoid causing her unnecessary pain. As Lloyd Livingston's wife, seeing the son of her enemies must have pushed her over the edge.

At his cousin's insistence he had gone home afterwards, but that had been unbearable. Keeping his distance had been the hardest thing he'd ever had to do. It had gotten so bad that, when he'd tried to go to bed in his mansion, he couldn't sleep. Every time he shut his eyes he saw Bethany's lifeless body on the kitchen floor. It had haunted him so much that he had gotten into his car, come back to the hospital, and stayed until he got word that Bethany had woken up. He hadn't slept in twenty-four hours, but he didn't care about that. Bethany was the only thing that mattered to him.

"I wanted to give her these." Without waiting for Elle's response, he walked over to the table beside Bethany's bed and set down the vase.

"Those are beautiful." Bethany gave him a tiny smile, lifting his spirits. If she could smile, then maybe she was out of the woods. Maybe the worst was over and she would have a full recovery. "Thank you."

She reached over and took his hand. Her hand was so small compared to his. So delicate.

He stared down at where their hands were joined and saw the tube that hooked her arm up to the IV bag. His chest tightened.

"You can leave now," her mother snapped, interrupting their moment.

"No, Mom," Bethany said firmly. "I want Kirk here."

"How is he even allowed in here?" her mother demanded. "He isn't family."

Arguing with her mother was going to get him nowhere. "I can go—"

"No," Bethany said, cutting him off. "You're not going anywhere. It isn't right for my mom to try to chase you away."

"Well, I'm not staying here with him," her mother spat out.

"Mrs. Livingston, I know our families have had our differences, but I care about your daughter," he said. "And because I care about her, I would like us to try to make peace. I don't have any negative feelings towards you."

"The only good thing about all of this is, at least now, your parents are getting a taste of their own medicine," Elle said, her voice full of venom. "I hope they both die in prison." After she spat those cruel words at him, she stormed out of the room and slammed the door behind her.

"Taste of their own medicine..." Her hold on his hand tightened. "I'm so sorry, Kirk, I don't know what my mother could have meant by that. As soon as she comes back I'm going ask her to apologize to you."

"Don't worry about that right now. Your mother is on edge, and I get that. The most important thing is for you to focus on getting better." He released her hand to take a seat beside her. "What she meant doesn't matter."

Bethany frowned, regarding him suspiciously. "There's something you aren't telling me."

Somehow, even through her injury, she knew him well enough now to know when he was holding back.

Yesterday he had rushed to her apartment to tell her about her father's arrest. Now, telling her the truth was the last thing he wanted to do. How could he add to her list of problems?

"My mom already told me about my father being arrested," she continued.

"I'm sorry." He paused, hearing the pain in her voice. "But I promise you that my cousin is working on it."

"Your cousin? You mean Ian?" She stared at him blankly. "Why would your cousin try to help my father get out of jail?"

"Well, he's helping my parents get out, but helping them helps your father."

"Your parents?" She let out a loud gasp. "Why would he need to help your parents? Don't tell me—"

"My parents were arrested yesterday," he said. "Along with your father."

Her hand flew up to her mouth. Clearly the news shocked her deeply. "Oh, no. Why were they arrested? Are they being accused of conspiring together?"

"The media keeps saying they're all co-conspirators. Which sounds crazy, doesn't it?" He sighed heavily. Somehow the gravity of the situation hadn't sunk in yet. He'd been so focused on Bethany that he had managed to temporarily push aside his concern for his parents. Now the concern was coming back and his insides churned. Anxiety didn't even begin to describe what he was feeling now. "Our parents are enemies, and yet it looks like they got arrested for conspiring to do something. I still can't figure out what they might have done."

"You don't know what the charges against them are?" she asked.

He shook his head. "No. My cousin called earlier today and said that the police department is keeping the details under wraps. So our parents probably know what the charges are, but that information hasn't leaked just yet."

"It's got to be something terrible." Hand shaking, she reached out to grab a hold of his arm. On any other day her touch would have soothed him. Dulled the ache raging inside him. Not today. Instead, her touch was like a condemnation. An indictment of him and his failure to protect her.

"My guess is another financial crime," he said.

"But how? My dad hasn't been out of prison for that long. Why would he risk going back?"

His eyes narrowed. "This is connected to Damien Kemp. He's the one thing that connects our parents. First he befriended your father so that he could launder money through the bank. When that had run its course, Kemp probably figure he'd get more by shaking down my parents."

"But we took care of Kemp. We made him a liability to the criminals he works for."

"Yeah, we did," he said. "The news even reported that Kemp skipped town yesterday. The same day that our parents got arrested. The same day you were attacked. That can't be a coincidence."

"You think Damien had something to do with my attack?"

"Of course. Wait..." He gave her a questioning look. "You must have seen your attacker, right? Or was he wearing a mask?"

"No. I mean, I don't know." She chewed her lip. "I can't remember the attack. The last thing I remember is taking Damien's money at the auction. Then I woke up in the hospital."

He didn't know which scenario would be easier for her: Remembering the details of something that terrifying, or not remembering and having to fight to recall what had happened. "Do the doctors know?"

She nodded. "They said my memory would come back eventually, but right now I can't remember what happened. My mother said that you called my brother with the news. You found me, didn't you?"

"I did." The ghost of an image flashed in his mind. A bleeding gash in her forehead. Blood running down into her blond hair. That sight would torment him until he made this right. Until he exacted his revenge on the man who had done this to her. "When I found you, I thought the worst had happened. I thought you were dead."

"You saved me," she breathed. "Even though you thought I might be dead, you saved me. Got me to the hospital in time so my injuries didn't leave permanent damage."

"I didn't save you," he bit out. "It was my fault you ended up here."

"Kirk, no. That's not true," she said firmly.

Convincing her that this was his fault while she recovered would be selfish. He refused to burden her with his guilt. The weight of that guilt had to rest on his shoulders. Not hers. Never hers.

If he had insisted that she stop investigating her father's alleged crimes, none of this would have happened. Instead of putting his foot down and keeping her safe, he had agreed to help her figure out if her father had been guilty of embezzling money. Worst of all, he had allowed her to meet with Damien Kemp. As San Diego's police chief, Kemp had been so powerful that even the mayor was afraid of him. Letting Bethany get mixed up with a man that dangerous was the worst mistake he had ever made. The mistake had nearly cost Bethany her life. Being wracked with guilt was the least he deserved for failing her.

"I'm going to find whoever did this to you," he said, a dark edge in his tone.

"Kirk, what are you saying?" She pulled her hand away from him and frowned. "You mean you want to put them in prison, right? That's all you want."

He balled his hands up into fists, his entire body shaking with rage. "No. Forget prison. I want to deal with them my way. In a way these goons will understand. If they're going to attack you, then I'm going to attack them."

Chapter 4

Fear forced the air out of her lungs.

Hearing Kirk say such things send a chill down her spine.

The expression on his face hardened. Fury blazed in his green eyes. His sensuous lips formed a harsh line. "This isn't something that can be solved with a simple time-out in jail. These people need to be dealt with."

"*These people?*" She shrank back and clutched the sheet again. When he had walked into her room, she had been desperate for comfort. Desperate for the safety of his arms. Now, she was more terrified of what he might do to her attacker than what her attacker might to do to her. "What do you mean?"

"It's obvious that Damien Kemp sent one of his goons after you," Kirk said. "The same way he sent one of his goons to make that threatening phone call and throw a brick at our window when we were at the resort. All at Kemp's instruction."

She swallowed hard. "But why? Don't these types of criminals usually kidnap or kill people? Why would they leave me alive?"

"I don't know. Thank bloody goodness they did."

"Kirk, please don't do anything reckless," she begged. "Just let the police handle this."

"We can't trust the police," he said firmly.

"Why not? Damien stepped down. He isn't the police chief anymore."

"The police have arrested our parents. Which means that, for all we know, Kemp's replacement might be just as bad as he was. The criminals that Kemp works for have the power to make sure another one of their puppets becomes chief of police," he explained. "The whole department could be filled with police officers who are loyal to Kemp and his agenda. How can we possibly trust them now?"

"We have to," she said. "What other choice do we have?"

"Let me and my cousin investigate this," he insisted.

She frowned, suddenly annoyed at how dismissive he sounded. "This concerns me. I was attacked, not you."

"Which is why I should help you find out who did this," he said. "You're in no state to be chasing after criminals."

"I thought we decided that you were going to stop being so overprotective." She folded her arms and scowled at him.

"We decided that before someone attacked you. Right now, I'm going to protect you whether you like it or not."

"And I have no say in the matter?"

"None whatsoever." His eyes narrowed. "I'm going to do what I should have been doing all along. Kemp and the criminals he answers to are still out there. Until I deal with them, I'm in charge of your security."

Her mouth fell open. "What does that mean? Do I have to ask your permission to do what I want?"

"Don't fight me on this, Bethany. You'll lose."

Annoyance twisted in her stomach. How dare he use his stubborn arrogance to try to control her. "You have no right to force me to do anything. I'm not a child."

"I'm not trying to force you," he said through clenched teeth. "But when you first met me, you really did have the right idea. I see that now. You were ready to fight for your family's honor."

When she first met Kirk, she lied about her identity. She hadn't told him that she was the daughter of the man his parents had sent to prison. It was easier to lie then. Anger and pain at losing her father had pushed her into making choices that she now regretted. "Lying to you and trying to get revenge was wrong. You weren't even responsible for my father going to prison."

"If I had been responsible for framing your dad for a crime he didn't commit, would you still think lying and trying to get revenge was wrong?"

"It's wrong no matter what," she said. "I learned to forgive the people who hurt me and my family."

"What if that forgiveness means the people who hurt you go on to hurt other people?" he asked. "What if the guy who attacked you does the same thing to someone else? What if they do something worse to an innocent person? What if the only way to stop that from happening is to lie? Or to choose revenge instead of justice? Would you let someone get hurt so that you could hold on to your newfound principles?"

"I..." Her voice trailed off. Right now, it felt like there was no right answer. Their parents had cut so many corners. Bent or even broken rules in their desperate rush for power and wealth. Even if their parents were innocent, they had worked with shady people. Made dangerous deals with less than reputable law firms. No matter how hard she had worked to get out of her father's shadow, his terrible choices still haunted her. His bad choices had dragged her wealthy family into poverty. Had turned her brother bitter and resentful. Had turned her mother into a shell of her former self. And they were still dealing with his bad choices ten years later.

That was why finding out the truth had been so important to her. Because, if she knew exactly what her father had done, she'd know what it would take to heal her family. To put her family back together again.

But even with her plan to investigate the truth with Kirk's help, some questions still remained. Though they had stopped a significant part of the shadiness going on at the bank her father had helped build and Kirk's parents now owned, they still hadn't unraveled the whole mystery. Still hadn't stopped all the criminals involved. Still hadn't figured out if her father really had embezzled all that money ten years ago. They had most of the dots, but they didn't know how it was all connected. And if someone else got hurt because of her single-minded desperation to solve the mystery, she didn't know how she'd ever live with herself.

Exhaustion settled over her. So bone-deep that she could no longer sit up. She shut her eyes for a second and lay back down on the bed. "I'm tired."

His hand gripped her shoulder. "Of course. I shouldn't have brought up all that painful stuff. Forgive me."

She sighed. "Just stay with me, please? Having you here makes me feel better."

"Then I'll stay until the doctors throw me out." He took her hand and brought her fingers to his lips. As his mouth brushed against her knuckles, warmth spread through her body. This was what she needed now. The security of his strength. Having him by her side meant that, maybe, everything would be all right.

———➤●◅———

KIRK SPENT THE REST of the day with her, while her mother came in occasionally to grumble and stare daggers at him. Eventually, it was time for them to leave her alone in her hospital room. Before Kirk left, he promised to visit the next day. A cold emptiness settled over her when they both finally left. She hated being alone in the room without her loved ones.

Soon, it was time for her to have her MRI scan, and once that ordeal was done she was taken back to her room to get some sleep.

By the time morning rolled around, she got an encouraging report about her MRI scan from Dr. Stavropoulos and he finally discharged her.

After Dr. Stavropoulos gave her a prescription for some pain medication, a nurse helped walk her out of her room and into the waiting room. A few days in bed had weakened her to the point that walking was difficult for her.

Her eyes widened when she noticed Kirk and her mother sitting side by side in stone-faced silence. Frankly, she was amazed her mother hadn't tried to attack him again.

"How are you feeling, kitten?" her mother asked as she approached them on shaky legs. "What did the doctor say?"

The nurse quickly said goodbye and left.

"I still feel a bit tired," Bethany said to her mother, "but my MRI scan came back and everything looks good."

"Oh, thank goodness." Her mother let out a loud sigh of relief. Thankfully, she looked sober this morning.

"That's the best news I've heard in weeks." Kirk stood up and wrapped his strong arm around her. "Let's get you home."

Her mother frowned. "You expect my daughter to go back to that awful apartment? The place where she was attacked?"

"No, I don't," Kirk said tightly. "She's coming home with me. To my place."

Bethany gasped. "I am? Kirk, we haven't discussed this. I can't intrude again—"

"You are not an intrusion." His tone was hard as granite. She'd heard that tone before, though he used it rarely. It meant there was no room for argument. Kirk's mind as made up and arguing with him was futile.

"What about all my things?" she asked weakly.

"My assistant will have them delivered to the mansion," he responded. "And don't worry about paying your rent, I'll take care of all that, too."

"Thank you so much, Kirk," Bethany said, touched by his generosity. "I can't stay at your place forever, though. I'll need to go back to my apartment eventually."

Her mother surged to her feet, alarm flashing in her eyes. "Bethany, you can't go back to that dreadful place. What if you're attacked again?"

"I can't believe I'm going to say this, but I agree with your mother," Kirk said. "Your apartment isn't safe, even if the attacker is arrested."

"For now it isn't." Bethany gave Kirk a meaningful look. "But when my attacker is caught, I will be moving back in. I'm not going to act like some fragile child who can't take care of herself."

"You can't stay with him!" her mother cried out. "You know you can't trust these Sterlings. Come and stay with me."

"Where are you staying?" Kirk asked. "From the little I know, you don't seem to have a permanent address, Mrs. Livingston."

Her mother scowled. "I'm sure her brother will let us move into his place."

As much as she hated the thought of overstaying her welcome at Kirk's mansion, staying with her family right now was only going to stress her out. They'd spend the entire time trying to talk her out of being with Kirk. Or they'd blame Kirk for her father's current predicament, and she didn't think she could handle that much drama while she was recovering from her injuries. Right now, it looked her like family was going to force her hand.

"Kirk has already offered, Mom," Bethany said gently, trying to smooth things over with her mother. "It wouldn't be right to turn him down when he's being so generous." She paused and looked at Kirk. "Can you give my mom your phone number so she can reach me? My cell phone is still at my apartment."

He nodded. "Of course. My number should be stored on your brother's phone. And I'll get you a new cell phone to use until you get your phone back."

Her mother glared at her. "I never thought you'd end up being the disloyal child, Bethany."

"Mom, please. Kirk is only trying to help."

"Mrs. Livingston, let's try to give Bethany some space here. She's been through one hell of an ordeal," Kirk said.

"And what about her father's ordeal? I don't know why I even came here." Her mother turned around and stormed out of the waiting room.

She swallowed the lump in her throat as she watched her mother disappear.

Kirk pulled his arm back and started to head after her mother.

Bethany grabbed hold of his arm. "Where are you going?"

"After her." His jaw clenched. "She has no right to talk to you like that. Not while you're recovering."

"Just let her go," she said softly. "My mom needs time to adjust to all this. That's all."

"We've been together for a while now. How long is it going to take for your family to adjust?" he demanded.

"They need time. This is difficult for them to understand."

"Did your brother even visit you in the hospital?" he asked.

She lowered her eyes, unable to meet his stern gaze. No, Joshua hadn't visited her. Hadn't even sent her flowers like her friend Naya had earlier that morning. She tried to tell herself that he hadn't reached out because he was so focused on saving their father. Somehow, she didn't believe that. Joshua still hadn't accepted her relationship with Kirk. The back of her eyes burned with unshed tears. "He didn't visit."

"You're joking! He's your family. Did any of your family besides your mother come?"

"Don't be angry with them," she pleaded in a small voice she didn't recognize. She couldn't stand the thought of him turning on her family right now.

"I can't promise that." He sighed and started to guide her out of the waiting room. "What I can promise is to get you home."

Half an hour later Kirk helped her out of his Mercedes and walked her up the walkway to the entrance of his mansion. His butler, Rath-bone, greeted them at the door and escorted them into the expansive living room.

"You can give Rathbone your prescription," Kirk told her. "He'll get it filled."

"Thank you, Rathbone. I really appreciate your help." She handed over the slip of paper and Rathbone gave her a small smile before he stepped out of the living room.

"The staff has stocked the guesthouse with food and tidied up the place. So everything is all ready for you," he said. "What do you want to do now? Eat? Sleep?"

"I just realized that I'm going to have to get in touch with my clients." There were still orders that she had to finish and deliver. If her clients had been trying to reach her for the past few days, they were probably frantic by now. Plus, she still needed to settle on a location for her shop.

"You're in no condition to do all that now," he said firmly. "I'll ask my assistant to take care of it. I can have her go down to your apartment within the next few days and she can contact your clients for you and buy some time with your orders."

"Kirk, she doesn't work for me. I can't expect her to do that," she said.

"I can either pay her extra or get another one of the executive assistants to do it," he said. "My staff can take care of anything."

It was easy to forget that he could do just about anything with a few commands. He was so powerful that he had people around him to do all the unexpected work. When her family had been wealthy it was exactly the same. Bethany hadn't had to lift a finger for herself until she turned seventeen.

She nodded, too exhausted to argue with him.

"My cousin Ian will be here soon to talk about our parents' legal case," he said. "Did you want to stick around to hear his update on the case or do you want to get some rest?"

"I could use a nap, honestly," she admitted.

He took her hand and started to walk with her across the living room to the patio outside.

The sensation of her hand in his made her heart squeeze. There was no way she could have survived this traumatic experience without him. As stubborn as he was, she knew he was only trying to protect her. If only her mother could see that.

Walking with him across his expansive property to the guesthouse only reminded her of just how bitter her mother must be. Her mother had lost her entire fortune. Kirk's wealth was a symbol of what her family had lost. It was only natural for her mother to resent him.

Maybe her family simply needed time. She hoped so. Because, as Kirk opened the guesthouse door for her, she remembered that there was a dream she had been holding on to for weeks now. It was more important than her dream of opening a fashion boutique. Probably even more important than discovering the truth about what happened ten years ago.

She followed him inside and he led her to the bedroom. The enormous bed was covered in pillows and she swept them aside to make room.

He helped pull the blanket aside as she settled into the bed.

The room smelled faintly of roses and the bed was as soft as a cloud. Kirk really had made sure everything was ready for her. If only her family could see this side of him. See how much he cared for her. He was always so attentive to her needs. Always so ready to see her taken care of.

"Thank you," she said softly as she shut her eyes.

Suddenly she felt the warmth of his lips kiss the corner of her mouth. She smiled against his lips in spite of all the turmoil she felt inside.

Right now, what she wanted most was for the feud between their families to end. She wanted to be with Kirk without having to deal with her mother's anger. Without her brother turning his back on her when she needed him most. Nothing would make her happier than having both the Sterlings and the Livingstons bury the hatchet long enough to put things right. Long enough to finally support her relationship with Kirk. A relationship that had already changed her life in ways she could never have expected.

But after her mother's outburst earlier today and with their parents in jail, that dream seemed impossibly out of reach.

Chapter 5

Several days later, he brought Bethany back to the mansion after her hospital visit. The doctor had removed her stitches and she was in good spirits. "Careful. Don't overexert yourself."

She gave him a faint smile. "I don't think there's a danger of that happening with you around to watch over me."

He supposed not, but seeing her so badly hurt had changed him. As much as he hated to admit it, her attack shifted something. Put the world into much clearer focus. They had enemies. Dangerous people who would do anything to keep both of their families in line. Bethany had almost paid with her life. He wasn't going to let her get hurt again.

While she settled into one of the plush chairs in the living room, he instructed a maid to bring some food.

It had been a long day. First he'd had to come up with a PR strategy at Sterling Investment Bank in the wake of his parents' arrest, and then afterwards he'd taken Bethany to the hospital. Now, all he wanted to do was spend time with her, but as he sat down across from her his cell phone buzzed.

He took his phone out of his jacket pocket and checked his messages. There was a new one from his assistant, which was probably important, so he took a look at it. As he skimmed over her message, his chest tightened. "Damn it."

"Is everything okay?"

"This is bad." He shoved his phone back into his pocket. How had he not anticipated this? "My assistant went to your apartment to get some of your things, but the place is crawling with cops."

"So, she can't bring my stuff?"

Kirk shook his head. "Not for the next several days. Your apartment is now a crime scene and the police have closed the place off. Nobody can get in while they gather evidence. Plus, they want to interview you as soon as possible."

"Well... it can't be that bad. I don't have anything to hide," she murmured.

"We can't trust the police," he reminded her. "Not with Damien Kemp still unaccounted for and our parents still in jail. The cops could be planting evidence or trying to cover something up."

Her face paled. "You don't think that Damien sent a *police officer* to attack me, do you? Do you really think other police officers are in on his schemes?"

"I don't know. Considering the shady people Kemp works for, there's a good chance that some of his goons are fellow police officers," he said. "They might already be doing his dirty work for him."

He had been so focused on her safety that he'd forgotten about keeping tabs on the police in case they searched her apartment. Now the cops were over there and he had no way of knowing what they were up to.

"Well, we can't ask them to stop looking for clues. That would look suspicious," she said.

She was right. Calling off the police was a risk they couldn't afford right now. Not with their parents back in prison.

A distant banging on the front door tore his attention from her. In the periphery of his vision he spotted his butler racing towards the mansion entrance.

Frowning, he got to his feet and followed after Rathbone to investigate. The last time there had been a commotion at his front door, the police had showed up to arrest Bethany on flimsy charges. He wasn't going to allow her to endure that kind of trauma ever again. This time he would force the police to arrest him instead of her.

Rathbone flung open the front door and a middle-aged man holding a microphone tried to push past him.

"Rathbone, what the hell is going on?" Kirk demanded.

"Sir, the guards at the front gate turned a group of reporters away. I have no idea how this gentleman got in."

The man struggled against Rathbone's surprising strength and held out the enormous microphone. "Mr. Sterling, I'm with the SDC News team—"

"I don't care." Kirk sauntered up to him and scowled. "Get the hell off my property."

"Hey, buddy, let go," the reporter snapped at Rathbone. "That's a thousand-dollar suit."

"Get out," Kirk said through gritted teeth.

"I just want to ask some questions about your parents' arrest," the reporter said, ignoring his anger. "Is this an end to the longstanding feud between your families? Did your parents and Lloyd Livingston commit some kind of crime together?"

Kirk took a step towards the reporter. "I don't need to answer this crap."

The reporter regarded him coolly and then smirked. "If you won't answer those questions, then maybe you'd like to answer some questions about Bethany Walker. There are rumors that Lloyd Livingston's daughter is right here on your property. This isn't the first time her father has been arrested. What's the nature of the relationship between you two? Were you in on your parents' crimes? Are more arrests imminent?"

Before Kirk could shout a string of obscenities, two burly guards appeared and grabbed the reporter roughly.

"We're sorry, Mr. Sterling," one of the guards said. "A bunch of reporters just showed up and we've taken care of them. But this guy managed to slip through because he and his cameraman scaled the back wall. The cameraman sprained his ankle, so the other guards are dealing with him."

"No!" the reporter yelled. "I have a right to know the truth. You can't do this to me."

The guards ignored his protests and dragged him away.

"Only a madman would try to climb that wall." Rathbone turned to give him a pained look. "I shall make sure that the guards have the matter taken care of." The butler stepped outside, shutting the front door behind him.

If the press was crazy enough to risk injury to get the story, then things were only going to get more intense. Since his parents' arrest reporters had jammed Sterling Investment Bank's phone lines, trying to get access. They'd even managed to get a hold of senior staff on their cell phones though, thankfully, his assistant had been able to field and intercept most of those calls to his cell phone. Nobody in the press had been able to get a hold of him. Yet. Which was probably why reporters had been driven to trespassing on his property.

"Kirk, is everything okay?"

He turned around at the sound of Bethany's voice.

She approached him, taking halting steps. Her injuries were still affecting her and she still wasn't moving with her usual energy. It pained him to stress her out with the details.

"Some reporters tried to get in, but security is handling it."

"Oh, no." She stumbled into his arms and buried her face in his shirt.

Her body trembled against him. Desperate to comfort her he wrapped his arms around her, holding her close. She tucked her head underneath his chin and his grip on her tightened as he pinned her to him. Just being able to hold her in his arms like this knocked him sideways. When he'd found her on the kitchen floor, the bleak terror of never seeing her alive again had almost destroyed him. The warmth of her body sent his heart racing. The sweet, feminine scent of her shampoo nearly undid him.

He held her trembling body for what must have been several minutes. Even without words, he sensed her pain and fear.

"It's happening again," she said, a tremor in her voice. "Reporters tried to get into my school when my dad was arrested the first time. They trailed me in their vans. I was so scared I'd end up saying the wrong thing. Something that might get my father into even worse trouble. Or make things even harder for my family."

She was only seventeen years old when the press had started to hound her. It wasn't fair to expect a teenage girl to answer for her father's sins. It wasn't fair then, and it wasn't fair now. Whatever her father was accused of now, Bethany had nothing to do with it. Trespassing on his property was bad enough, but dragging her name through the mud sent a wave of white-hot anger crashing through him.

"They have no right to harass you," he ground out. "My lawyer will be in touch with that TV station."

"Did...did they know I was here?" she asked. "I think I heard that reporter mention my name."

"Yes, they knew." He kissed the top of her head, the urge to protect her so strong he could barely stand it. "I don't know how they knew. Someone must have leaked that information to the press."

"But who could have told them?" she asked. "Only your staff knows."

"My staff would never leak that kind of information." Everyone who worked at the mansion had been thoroughly vetted and had worked on the property for months or years. Their loyalty was absolute. He paid them well enough to know that no TV station would ever get them to talk.

"Wait." She pulled back and looked into his eyes. "My mother knows I'm here."

Kirk frowned. He didn't know Elle Livingston well enough to know if she was capable of betraying her daughter like this. The thought of her throwing her own daughter to the press made his blood boil. It was unimaginable that a parent could do that to their child, and yet it made sense. "Is she the kind of person who would leak your location to the media?"

"Ten years ago, I would have said no." She lowered her eyes like she was too distraught to hold his gaze and heaved out a sigh. "But she's been a heavy drinker on and off for years now. I don't know what she's capable of doing if she needs cash to buy alcohol. Losing the family fortune has made her capable of a lot of things." She turned away, turning her back to him as her shoulders heaved.

Seeing her in so much pain hurt him more than anything. Because, even though he might be able to protect her from overzealous reporters, he had no idea how to put her family back together for her. Without thinking, he reached out to her and gripped her shoulders.

"My family has abandoned me." Her breath hitched. "I feel so alone."

He released her shoulders to spin her around to face him again. He then gently cupped her face to get a better look at her. Bethany's eyes were shining and her lower lip trembled.

"I'm here with you," he told her. "No matter what."

He'd barely gotten the words out before she planted a kiss on his lips. She ghosted her mouth across his, the kiss both hesitant and tender. There was an anguish in the kiss as she took hold of his shirt and gripped him for dear life.

Kirk wrapped his arms around her small waist and pinned her against his body. Anchored her against him so that she knew she was safe with him. He hadn't kissed her like this since he'd found her in the kitchen. They hadn't been intimate since before her attack either. When he'd realized that she would recover from her injuries, Kirk had vowed to give her as much time as she needed. Give her the space to heal. If he had to wait for eternity to have her body again he would wait.

Which was why, as she deepened the kiss, he let her lead. Let her set the pace while he kept the kiss as tender as possible. She tasted sweet, her full lips impossibly soft.

Her tongue met his, sending hot desire straight to his groin. She quivered beneath his fingertips and he wrestled with his arousal. His blood smoldered through his veins. He had to keep his carnal desire in check. Right now, he had to give her the tenderness she needed.

Their tongues entwined and she moaned softly before pulling away. Her blue eyes glowed with soft a warmth, though there was still sadness in them. A sadness he would give his life to chase away.

"Take me to your bedroom," she said softly. "Take me upstairs."

"Are you sure? There's no pressure here," he assured her. "We don't have to do anything while you're still healing."

She gave him a faint smile. "I want to do this. I want you. Besides, now that my stitches are out the doctor said I can have sex without any problems."

His eyebrows shot up in surprise. "You asked your doctor that?"

"Yes." A slight blush crept up her cheeks. "I've missed being with you."

"I've missed being with you, too." He reached out to caress her cheek, and her blush deepened. "We can take this as slow as you want, okay?"

"Okay." The sadness in her eyes turned into adoration. That look turned his insides to molten lead. Bethany still trusted him. He didn't know what he'd done to earn her faith in him, especially after he'd opened her up to so much danger, but he wasn't going to let her down ever again.

Reaching for his hand, she leaned into him to plant a quick kiss on his lips.

His thumb brushed against her wrist and he felt her quickening pulse.

With their fingers laced together, he guided her upstairs until they reached his bedroom.

He closed the door and watched as she approached his bed. The way she moved intoxicated him. Every movement was graceful and sensual. The inviting sway of her hips made his mouth water. As the hem of her dress swirled right above her knees, those long, shapely legs were already distracting him.

One coy glance over her shoulder and he was gone. Too aroused to say anything coherent, he stepped over to her and seized her hips.

Her mouth was on his again and he groaned at the sensation of her perfect mouth on his. Slowly, he ran his tongue across her lips and she parted them, letting him in. He swirled his tongue into her mouth, taking his time to savor her. Nothing could ever taste as good. Kissing her was heaven on earth.

She pulled back to remove her dress and tossed it onto the floor. Her lacy black bra and matching panties contrasted with her creamy white skin.

Burning with the need to touch her again, he let his hands roam up from her waist until he was cupping the two soft orbs of her breasts. With a breathy moan she arched her back, pushing her magnificent breasts against the palms of his eager hands.

He thumbed her nipples through the flimsy lace, her body trembling as she reached behind her to unhook her bra. The fabric slipped away from her, revealing her full breasts.

With a lift of her chin, she met his gaze. Despite the blush in her cheeks, she didn't look away. This was her opening herself up to him. Letting him drink his fill of her perfect body.

Seeing her pink nipples left him painfully, desperately aroused. "I will never get tired of looking at you," he told her. "You're the most beautiful woman I've ever seen."

That elicited a smile that reached her eyes, setting them on fire until they were a pair of blue flames. Wordlessly she climbed onto the bed and peeled off her black panties.

She was too tempting. If he didn't get out of his clothes quickly to join her soon he was going to explode. In what felt like seconds, he stripped out of his clothes and got into bed with her.

He lay down beside her, tracing a hand across her exposed skin. Skin as soft and smooth as silk. His fingertips skimmed up her supple thigh, across her stomach, until he reached her breasts.

Kirk traced his fingers along the swell of one of her breasts and she inhaled audibly.

The fire in her eyes burned even brighter, spurring him on to let his hand wander up her slender neck until he was dragging his thumb across her quivering lower lip.

It was then that his gaze drifted up from her glistening mouth to her forehead. There, on her perfect skin, was a faint, nearly invisible scar from the gash she'd been given by the coward he wanted to get his hands on and kill. If he hadn't memorized every inch of her body he probably wouldn't have even noticed the scar, but Kirk could see it.

Anguish tore at his heart. Someone had put their hands on his Bethany. She was everything to him. Everything. His life. His world. And the person who was responsible for nearly taking her away from him was still out there.

She must have noticed the anger in his eyes because she reached out, planting her hand on his cheek. "Hey, don't disappear on me now. I'm right here. You reminded me that I'm not alone. Neither are you."

What had he done to deserve this woman? A woman who always knew how to chase away the pain in his heart.

He pressed a kiss to her lips, enjoying the sensation of her soft mouth on his. "Are you ready for me?"

"More than ready," she said, her voice slightly teasing. "If I don't have you right now I'm going to go crazy."

Kirk flashed her a knowing smile before lowering himself onto her.

Suddenly, her long legs wrapped around his waist, and she guided him in.

With her guidance and one quick thrust, he was inside her, enveloped by her tight wetness. He groaned as pleasure gripped him. Nothing would ever feel this good. Burying himself inside the woman he had thought he'd lost.

She let out a loud cry of ecstasy. Her arms wrapped around his shoulders and he looked down at her eyes. They were clouded with pleasure. And something else flickered in them for a moment. Trust. Her trust in him was so complete that mere days after her injury she was opening herself up to him. Giving him her all.

He would never ever take her trust for granted. In that moment, with their bodies joined, Kirk vowed to always fight to be worthy of that trust.

She clenched around him, driving more pleasure through his body. The sensation of her wet warmth clamping down on him was so incredible it ripped his breath away. Aching to give her more pleasure he rocked into her, coaxing a ragged moan from her throat.

As he sped up the pace of his thrusts, he captured her lips in a searing kiss. She writhed beneath him, digging her nails into his back. The sweet pain spurred him on and he tore his lips away, fisting the sheets as he pleasured her with powerful strokes. She whimpered. Moaned his name.

The sound of his name on her lips dragged him to the brink of ecstasy and he groaned his release as his climax slammed through him. She came right after him—loud, breathless cries signaling her orgasm.

Reluctantly, he rolled away from her. The absence of her touch for even a second was maddening to him. Needing her, he pulled her close and she lay her head down on his chest.

She sucked in deep breaths and they lay together as they tried to get their breathing under control.

Finally she spoke, her voice hoarse from their lovemaking. "That was even more amazing than I remembered."

He grinned and lazily started to stroke her silky hair. "You were incredible."

A buzz from his cell phone dragged his attention from her and he sighed. The real world was trying to distract him from her. "That's probably my assistant again. Maybe she has an update on the situation with the police."

Bethany moved back as he heaved himself off the bed to fish his cell phone out of his jacket pocket. The problem with the police probably had to be handled. And fast. If the police department was compromised, he was going to need to get Bethany a good lawyer. And he needed an update on his parents. So far the police weren't saying anything, and the recent update from his cousin Ian hadn't revealed all that much. If they had any hope of saving his parents and protecting themselves from the police, they were going to need a strategy.

Kirk looked at his messages, his eyebrows going up in surprise.

"Who was it?" she asked.

"Maybe your faith in your family wasn't so misplaced after all," he answered, holding out his cell phone to her. "It was your brother. He says he wants to talk. Right now."

Chapter 6

Bethany tried to chase away her jitters as she put on fresh clothes that the mansion staff had brought her. She glanced at herself in the mirror of her bedroom, making sure she looked presentable. Even though she had been injured she didn't want to worry her brother, so she wanted to look as healthy as possible.

With her apartment closed off as a crime scene she didn't have all that many of her own things, so she had to make do with whatever Kirk's staff brought her. Satisfied that she looked healthy enough, she headed out of the guesthouse and back to the main house.

Kirk was sitting in the living room, sending messages on his phone. He glanced up at her. "I'm giving your brother directions. It sounds like he's just a few minutes away."

Her stomach tightened. Joshua would be here soon. Though she had talked to him infrequently on the phone over the past several weeks, she hadn't seen him. No doubt he still hadn't forgiven her about being with Kirk. Which made her wonder why he even wanted to see her in the first place.

It had to be about their father. She forced down a breath, more anxious about her father's situation than she had ever been. What if Joshua was here to tell her even worse news about their dad?

She settled down to sit on the sofa and turned on the TV to distract herself. Her brother was going to be here any minute, and the last time Joshua and Kirk had been in the same place together it had almost come to blows. Joshua could be impulsive. A hot-head when angry. Kirk was far less impulsive, but he had an over- protective streak. If her brother lashed out at her, Kirk was liable to try to defend her honor with his fists.

Before she could open her mouth to warn him about fighting with her brother, Kirk stood up and shoved his phone back into his pocket. "Your brother just drove past the front gate."

Too anxious to speak, she stood up and followed Kirk out of the living room to the front door. The butler was already at the door and he opened it to let her brother in.

Seeing Joshua sent a swirling storm of emotions through her. She was elated that he seemed to want to see her after her ordeal. But part of her was filled with trepidation that his motives for seeing her might be because of something catastrophic.

Her brother looked exhausted, with bloodshot eyes and unkempt dark hair. "Hi, Bethany." Joshua ignored Kirk's outstretched hand to walk over to her and give her an awkward hug.

"Hi, Josh." She took a step back to really look at her brother. There was more than just exhaustion etched on his face. A face that looked so much like their father's. The exhaustion was mixed with hopelessness. A dejection she'd never seen from him before.

Her brother glanced around, taking in the opulence of the mansion with a curled lip. "Nice place. I can see why you'd shack up with Sterling."

"Aren't you going to say hello to Kirk?" she asked pointedly.

Joshua focused his attention on Kirk, who right now was obviously suppressing a scowl. "You and I are going to need to talk, Sterling."

"My relationship with Bethany isn't up for discussion," Kirk warned.

"Let's set that aside," her brother said. "For now."

"Fine with me," Kirk said in a harsh tone.

"Have you got a bathroom?" Joshua asked.

"Head through the living room and it's the third door on the right," Kirk replied.

Joshua gave a curt nod and headed out of sight.

Kirk scowled. "That brother of yours is something else."

"You could probably say that about my whole family," she murmured.

"Well, look on the bright side. We haven't started punching each other yet," Kirk said with a sardonic chuckle.

She smiled in spite of her apprehension. "I'm going to take that as a minor victory."

"I'll go make sure the kitchen staff is working on refreshments for your brother," he said.

"I do need to take my medication, so I'll go with you." She took his hand and walked with him to the gourmet kitchen.

Once she gulped down some water with her medicine, she followed Kirk back to the living room. Her brother was seated on one of the sofas, looking around at the room with the same resentment she'd had when she first came to Kirk's seaside mansion. If her brother was willing to endure Kirk's wealth after their family's downfall, it was clear that he needed to discuss something important. She only hoped that Kirk and her brother took this chance to hear each other out, instead of continuing their families' never-ending feud.

"SO, WHAT DID YOU WANT to talk about, Joshua?" Kirk sat down on the sofa beside Bethany and gave her brother a hard stare.

Joshua met his stare with a scowl. "It's about my dad," Joshua muttered. "His bail was denied."

"Oh, no." She clutched her chest, a mournful expression on her face. "What have they charged him with? What can we do, Joshua? I gave Mom a list of contact details for some lawyers who can help Dad, but there's got to be more that we can do."

"This whole time I've been running around trying to raise funds for bail and they turned his bail down." Joshua shook his head angrily.

"What does this mean for Kirk's parents?" she asked.

He was supposed to be getting an update from his cousin later today but if Joshua had news, he wanted to hear it. "Have the police said what our parents are even being charged with?"

"Only my dad had been denied bail so far." Joshua swallowed hard before narrowing his eyes at him. "I guess your parents' fancy lawyer might get them out of this while my father rots." The bitterness in his tone echoed off the living room walls.

As much as he disliked Joshua, the guy had a point. It wasn't fair that Lloyd Livingston was getting harsher treatment because he was no longer wealthy. The system was unjust, and even though that put Kirk at an advantage it still rankled.

"I don't know what the charges are," Joshua added. "I've been talking to the public defender representing my father, and he says the cops are keeping this under wraps. It looks like they're using our parents to go after someone bigger and they don't want that getting out. They don't want whoever the person is to catch wind of the investigation and skip town."

"Are you sure that's the reason they aren't publicly revealing the charges?" Kirk asked.

Joshua frowned. "I'm not completely sure, but what other reason would they have?"

"I can't go into the reasons right now, but I'm going to advise you not to trust the police department. I'd also advise you to pass that on to your father. Out of all of us, your father is the one who really needs to keep an eye on what the cops might be up to," Kirk explained. If Damien Kemp was angry with him and Bethany, that rage would definitely extend to their families. Though Joshua was kind of an ass, he deserved to know what he was dealing with when it came to the police department.

Her brother snorted. "Cops ruined my family, remember? You don't have to tell me twice."

"I'm serious," Kirk said firmly. "Don't trust them and don't give them more information than you have to."

"Okay. I get it."

"What can we do?" Bethany asked. "There has to be a way to help Dad."

"There is," Kirk said. "It's clear that a public defender isn't going to be good enough. Your father needs to have a solid, capable attorney."

"I don't know if you know this, Sterling, but my dad can't afford something like that," Joshua bit out. "While your parents get to enjoy all the money my dad made through hard work, my old man will be rotting away in jail for who knows what reason."

She chewed her lip anxiously. "Josh, please—"

"You know it's true, Bethany," her brother said, cutting her off sharply.

"I'll pay for your father's attorney," Kirk said.

Surprise flashed in Joshua's eyes. "What? Are you serious? Why the hell would you offer to help me?"

"I'm not doing it for you," Kirk said coldly. "I'm doing it for Bethany. For some reason, she still believes in your father. Even after the things he's been accused of. Even after he callously disowned her and left her to fend for herself. If Bethany can still have faith in him after all this time, the least I can do is try to help him."

Bethany shook her head vigorously. "No, Kirk. I'm grateful for your offer, but you've already done so much for me."

"Then what will it hurt to help you out now?" he asked gently.

"Even if I agreed to this, there's no way my father would accept money from you," she said. "He'd never forgive us if we paid for his lawyer with money from a Sterling."

"You're telling me that your father is so proud he'd be willing to remain behind bars to prove a point?"

"My father disowned me for dating you," she reminded him. "He wouldn't hesitate to turn the money down. Tell him, Josh."

Her brother scratched the stubble on his jaw thoughtfully. "That's true. Dad can be a stubborn ass. He's too proud to take money from his enemies."

Bethany nodded. "See?"

"But we don't have to tell him where the money came from," Joshua went on. "We could say Bethany paid for the lawyer."

"If he wouldn't accept money from Kirk, I doubt he'd take money from me," she said.

"Good point." Joshua paused for a moment. "I've been trying to raise money for my dad's bail. I haven't had to collect it since his bail got turned down, but what if I told him that's how I got the money?"

"How have you been raising bail funds anyway?" she asked.

Joshua shrugged. "Old friends and associates."

"Associates?" She raised an incredulous eyebrow.

"Dad's old prison buddies." Joshua grimaced.

She gasped. "What? You've been trying to raise money by going to hardened criminals?"

Chapter 7

"**I**'m doing what I need to do to save my father," Joshua said, his tone icy.

Kirk shot him a warning glare. He sure as hell wasn't going to let Joshua disrespect Bethany in his own home. Especially not while she was recuperating.

"*Our* father," she corrected him.

Joshua's eyebrow quirked up. "What?"

"He's our father," she repeated with a lift of her chin. "I care about him, too, Josh. Even though he wants nothing to do with me, I'm going to fight for him. I'm going to help him whether you like it or not."

Her brother scowled. "If you want to help Dad, don't question my methods."

"You're not going to talk to your sister like that here," Kirk said, fighting to keep his voice as calm and even as possible. "You will respect her. Don't make me say it again."

Joshua frowned. "You're lucky this is your house, Sterling."

"Luck has nothing to do with it," Kirk fired back. "I earned this property. You can either hear your sister out or you can leave."

"Maybe I *should* leave—"

"I'll remind you that you're the one who showed up here uninvited," Kirk said.

Bethany raised her hands. "Please don't argue. Let's all try to listen to each other."

Trust Bethany to be the peacemaker. The voice of reason. For her sake he would try to keep his temper in check. He just hoped that Joshua would try to do the same.

"Clearly, your sister doesn't think it's a good idea to be asking ex-cons for money," Kirk said. "There's a lot of risk involved with owing those types of people a favor."

Joshua sighed. "Look, I know that. I'm not stupid. But it's the only way I knew to save my father. What would you do to save your parents now that they're in jail, too, Sterling?"

Kirk went silent for a long moment. His parents' arrest had come as a complete shock. It was such a surprise that he was still grappling with it. Still trying to accept it as the new normal. Part of him was devastated for them, while the other part of him was angry with them. How could they have allowed themselves to get into a mess like this? What law had they broken? "Honestly? As pissed as I am with them, I'll do anything for my parents."

"Are you saying I don't care enough about my father?" Bethany asked in surprise.

"That's not what I'm saying," Kirk replied. "I don't think there's anyone in the world who loves their father more than you do, Bethany. What I'm saying is that, while I understand why you'd hesitate to ask criminals for bail money, I also understand why your brother would do it. You're both in a tough position. There's no right or wrong here. Not in a situation like this."

While he was apprehensive about his own parents, he was also concerned for Lloyd Livingston. He didn't like Bethany's father, but he was still pissed that Livingston was probably going to get far worse treatment than his own parents. All because of privilege and wealth. However, Kirk tried not to feel too sorry for Lloyd; after all, he had gotten a lenient prison sentence on account of his status just ten years ago.

Kirk forced out a sigh. Things were just as unfair now as they had been a decade ago. That much hadn't changed.

She bit her lip, clearly taking in his words. "So, what do we do?"

If they were going to give her father a chance to get out of jail, Kirk was going to have to take charge. Bethany was still recuperating, and he could see how stressful the situation was for her. It was his job to make things as easy as possible while she recovered. "The best plan is for me to pay for a better lawyer for your father. With that done, your brother can tell him that it came from some of his prison buddies."

"Do we really have to lie to my dad?" She frowned and turned her attention to Joshua. "He's already angry with me for being with you, Kirk. Who knows what he'll do if he finds out what Josh has done."

"I'll take the risk," her brother said firmly. "Our only chance to get Dad out of jail is to appeal the bail ruling. A better lawyer can take on the judge and get Dad home. Dealing with his anger when he finds out where the money really came from is a small price to pay to get him out."

"That's easy for you to say. He hasn't disowned you." Her voice was small. Lost and tinged with sadness.

"If things go according to plan he'll disown me, too." Joshua forced a smile. "Maybe you can get some sympathy points from Dad when you tell him about being in the hospital."

"Maybe..." She looked down at her hands, which were now clasped.

Kirk reached out and placed a hand on her shoulder, desperate to comfort her. Her strained relationship with her father still hurt her, no matter how brave she tried to be about it.

Her brother paused, obviously noticing her shift in demeanor. "I'm sorry I didn't visit you in the hospital. I was so focused on getting Dad out of jail. Plus, Mom was with you and I thought that would make things easier."

"It didn't," she murmured.

"Did Mom get drunk or something?" her brother asked. "Because she promised to lay off the booze while she looked after you."

"She didn't drink while I was in the hospital," she responded. "It's just that she was really upset about Kirk being there. And it hurt a lot to see her get angry about him being there."

"We're all hurting," Joshua said dismissively.

Anger flared in him at the way Joshua seemed to minimize Bethany's pain. "Your sister was attacked and you and your family have spent the entire time antagonizing her over old wounds. You haven't asked her how she's doing. Or how she's coping. That's messed up, even for you."

Joshua ran his hand through his hair and blew out a frustrated breath. "So, how are you doing, Bethany?"

"I got my stitches taken out today," she answered.

"Was it a robbery gone wrong or something?" Joshua asked. "Did your attacker take anything?"

"I don't think so," she said.

"The police are going through her apartment," Kirk explained. "So her place will probably be closed off for a couple of days while they gather evidence."

"Didn't you say not to trust the police?" Joshua asked.

"We don't, but we don't have a choice with this," Kirk replied.

A maid appeared, balancing a tray of refreshments in her hands.

"Oh, food and drinks are here." Bethany stood up to take the tray from the maid, who quickly walked out of the living room.

Her brother abruptly got to his feet. "I should go. Don't want to take up any more of your time."

"Are you sure? Don't you want to eat before you go?" Sadness flashed in her eyes as she set the tray down on the coffee table.

"No, thanks. I've already asked for too much," her brother said with a grimace.

"You can choose a lawyer from the list Bethany gave your mother," Kirk said. "I'd help you decide, but considering your father can't know about me paying for his lawyer it's best I stay out of this as much as possible."

Joshua nodded. "Yeah, I agree. How do we deal with paying the lawyer?"

"I'll get my assistant to transfer the money to you," Kirk said.

For the first time, Joshua smiled. "I... honestly, Sterling, I don't know what to say other than thank you. When this is all over, I'll work on paying you back. Even though we're enemies, I want to do the right thing here."

"Don't bother with that. All that matters is that your father gets the same chance as my parents."

Joshua approached his sister and hugged her. "Thanks, Bethany. Guess Dad owes you one, even though he doesn't know it yet."

She hugged him back. "Just take care of yourself, okay?"

"I will. And I'll be in touch to let you know how things are going with Mom and Dad. I'll see myself out." With that he released his sister, gave Kirk a curt nod, and walked out.

Bethany resumed her seat, the expression on her face now inscrutable. "I can't believe Josh said he was going to pay you back. It's the most grown up thing he's ever done."

"He did seem different," he admitted. "I mean, he's still kind of a hothead, but he obviously wants to help your father."

Slowly, her lips turned up into a smile. "Maybe this means that he's finally growing up. Taking on responsibility after all these years."

"I think you being in the hospital has something to do with it. You weren't around to take care of everything like you usually are, so he had to do his part for once," Kirk said. "You're usually the one who looks out for everyone, aren't you?"

She nodded. "After Dad went to prison, I took care of my family as best as I could. I looked out for Josh. Helped my mom when she got drunk. I even took on temp jobs when she got too drunk to function. All while I was in high school. Then, during college, I did everything from babysitting jobs to designing clothes while I was in Italy, and sent money home whenever I could."

He took her hand and squeezed it affectionately. "That's a lot for anyone to handle, much less a teenager."

"Yes, it was a lot. However, this is giving me hope. If Josh can step up like this, then who knows what else might happen. Ending up in the hospital wasn't a good thing, obviously, but if this is the silver lining I'll take it."

"And you still don't remember what happened?" he asked gently.

She shook her head. "No memories yet."

"Well, it was either Damien Kemp or one of his goons," Kirk said. "It was probably his way of trying to intimidate you."

"Would he really go through all that trouble, though? Intimidating me after we took back some of the money he's laundered seems like the last thing he should have been focusing on. You'd think Damien would have wanted to leave town as quickly as possible before his bosses found out about all the money he lost."

"Ordinarily I'd say we can always wait on what the police find, but we can't trust them," he muttered. "They might be trying to hide Damien's tracks at this very moment, for all we know."

"I wish my memory would come back."

He squeezed her hand again, noticing how small and fragile it seemed. "Don't rush it. The doctor said it would come back eventually. Try to focus on the things you can control."

"Well, now that we figured out a way to help my dad, what are you going to do about your parents?" she asked.

"Based on what my cousin has told me, my parents have the top lawyers in the city working for them. Right now, the best thing I can do for my parents is figure out what they've been charged with. And I'm going to need to get more control of the bank in their absence." While Bethany had been healing, he hadn't been nearly as focused on Sterling Investment Bank as he would usually have been. Because, no matter how important the bank was, Bethany was way more important to him.

"How are you going to get more control?" she asked. "Doesn't your dad still need to approve your decisions?"

"He does." Which was why Kirk wanted to put someone temporarily in charge of the bank. Ordinarily, he'd take over his father's position as bank president, but his father would never agree to it. His dad had done everything in his power to keep Kirk from taking over the bank from him before he was ready to hand it over. Making even a temporary play for president now would start a crisis with his father and the board members who were still loyal to him. The best thing to do was to give someone else that acting-president role until his parents got out of jail.

"In a couple of days I'm going to suggest that the board put in a temporary replacement for my dad. I'll have to pick someone loyal to my father if I want to get my dad to sign off on the plan," he explained.

"Have you decided who should take over your dad's position?" she asked.

He nodded. "I have, though I have to swear you to secrecy. You can't tell anyone."

"I promise I won't tell," she said. "I know how important it is to keep a lid on information in the corporate world."

"I've been narrowing it down over the past couple of days. The candidates for the position have been sending e-mails, practically begging for the job. Right now it's down to Rod Mason and Pierce Turner."

"Uncle Pierce? He was a senior executive when my father ran the bank." She sighed sadly. "Dad and Uncle Pierce were best friends. They went to college together. Except, after Dad's arrest, he turned his back on us. Pretended not to know us anymore."

"I'm sorry."

"It hurt because Uncle Pierce is my godfather," she said softly. "Or at least he was. I doubt he still sees himself that way."

"I hate to tell you this, but I can't let anything personal influence my decision," he said. "The employees at SIB are counting on me to choose the right person to weather this storm."

"I understand. I'd never expect you to make a decision for the bank based on my feelings. Besides, Uncle Pierce would probably be a good choice."

He admired how fair she was in spite of her own pain. If more businesses were run by fair-minded people like her, the world would be a much better place. "SIB would be in good hands with him," he agreed. "I just hope it isn't too late to make a decision like this. We've got a good PR strategy going about my parents getting arrested, but things are still pretty chaotic right now."

Concern flickered in her eyes. "You've been so focused on me that you haven't had the chance to pay attention to the bank. What are you going to do with everything going on with your parents?"

"I've focused on you because you're the most important part of my life." He gazed at her, his heart starting to race as their eyes met. When he'd found her on her kitchen floor he'd worried that he wouldn't even get the chance to ever look into her eyes again. Just being with her now was more than he could have ever dreamed of in that awful moment.

She smiled before leaning over to press a kiss to his lips. "You are the most wonderful man in the world. What did I do to deserve you?"

Kirk cupped her cheek gently and returned her smile. "Guess we both got lucky." He only hoped their luck would last long enough to find her attacker and set their parents free.

Chapter 8

A crowd of reporters was trying to force its way into Sterling Investment Bank's entrance.

Kirk cursed under his breath as he approached the raucous crowd. "Can't you get rid of them?" he asked the security guards flanking him.

"Sorry, Mr. Sterling, but as long as they stay out of the building they have the right to be here," one guard said.

"They're trying to get in," he pointed out.

"They're not going to get inside," the other guard assured him. "Security has been beefed up. Don't worry, sir, they're not going to get in."

Maybe they wouldn't, but he still had to walk through a crowd of these people to get to work. Not to mention bank clients having to deal with the chaos that was sure to turn them away, if his parents' arrest hadn't already.

A photographer in the crowd pointed right at him. "There he is!"

As Kirk started to elbow his way through the crowd, TV cameras and microphones were shoved in his face. Cameras flashed as photographers eagerly took photos of him. He kept his face as placid as possible, knowing that every single thing he did right now was going to be under a microscope to be dissected by everyone in town. The bank needed him to project as much calm and strength as possible. Their shareholders were counting on him to get this right.

Finally, he forced his way through the bank entrance and headed for the elevator, leaving his security detail behind. The guards would guard him to and from the bank, but he had insisted they give him his space while he worked. There was nothing more obnoxious than an executive who brought security with him everywhere he went.

Once he got to his office, he went over the day's itinerary with his assistant Camille.

"You only have one meeting scheduled for today, sir." Camille swiped her fingers across her tablet. "Though you're also scheduled to make a conference call with our office in Berlin in twenty minutes."

"Right. Thanks for the reminder, Camille," he said as he sat at his desk. "I'd like you to call my brother in New York for any updates from the New York office."

"Will do, sir," she said with a nod.

A knock on his office door dragged his focus away. He frowned. "Am I expecting anyone this early?"

"Oh, I was just about to get to that, Mr. Sterling," Camille said. "Someone from cyber security is here to do a sweep of all your devices. The cyber security team thought it would be a good idea, in light of everything going on with your parents." She gave him a sympathetic look.

"Okay, let them in." He sighed and raked his hand through his hair. If cyber security thought they needed to do a sweep, they obviously thought they had reason to. Nobody knew what his parents were being accused of, and that unknown meant SIB was vulnerable. He didn't want to condemn his parents by assuming their guilt, but if they had worked with shady characters like Damien Kemp they might have been desperate enough to put the bank in real danger. As annoying as dealing with tech delays might be today, it was better to be safe than sorry.

Camille headed over to his office door to open it. "Mr. Sterling, Edward Pryce is here. He's one of our network and security officers. You remember Edward, don't you, sir?"

A tall man sporting a huge pair of glasses walked in.

Though he prided himself on learning about his employees, cyber security wasn't usually on his radar. Kirk appraised Edward for a second and realized that he actually did look familiar. "Yes, I remember now."

Edward smiled at Camille. "Hey, Camille. Nice to see you again."

Camille blushed faintly and she hurried out of the room. The hurrying away was uncharacteristic of his meticulous assistant, so Edward must have had some sort of effect on her. That brought a smile to Kirk's face. Despite his parents being in jail, it would be good for his employees to find some kind of happiness.

"Hey, Mr. Sterling." Edward walked closer and held out his hand. "Kind of flattering that you remember me."

Kirk shook his hand. "You've been with us for a long time haven't you, Edward?"

"Yup. I've been at the bank for over ten years." Edward beamed proudly.

"You don't look a day over twenty-five," Kirk said with a raised eyebrow.

Edward laughed and pushed his glasses up his nose. "I get that all the time. I'm thirty, sir. Started working here when it was the Livingston Bank. Lloyd Livingston himself hired me right after I graduated. You know I started college when I was fifteen years old, right?"

"That's impressive."

Edward puffed out his chest. "Thanks, sir. That means a lot coming from you."

"Guess you want me to get out of your way," Kirk said, getting up.

"Sorry about the inconvenience, but safety has to come first." Edward walked by him to reach down and boot up the laptop on his desk. "I need all your devices. Phones, tablets, anything you've got."

"Edward, I can't live without my phone," Kirk said.

"How about I take care of that first, so that you can have it for the rest of the day?"

"Sounds good. Thanks, Edward."

Fifteen minutes later, Edward handed back his cell phone and Kirk left him to finish his work.

Since it was almost time for his morning meeting, Kirk stepped out of his office and ducked into a conference room.

Soon, a handful of the bank's most senior executives, investors, and shareholders gathered in the meeting room with him and sat at the large table by the glass wall. Among them were one of his father's lawyers, and his cousin Ian. While Ian didn't work at SIB, he was one of the bank's youngest shareholders. Plus, Kirk trusted his cousin.

After a brief greeting they all took their seats.

"Before we get started I'd just like to hand out a copy of this statement from President Sterling." His father's lawyer started to hand out printed documents. "It states that, while you can discuss and choose a candidate for this temporary decision, Bruno Sterling will ultimately make the final decision. It also states that he approves of the salary that the chosen candidate will be allotted."

"Fine," Kirk said with a nod. "I've narrowed down choices for the temporary position of bank president to Rod Mason and Pierce Turner. Obviously none of this can leave the room. If the media gets wind of our plans for a temporary replacement they could leak the information and force our hand. Or worse, embarrass the candidate we don't end up choosing. SIB's reputation is at stake here, and so are the careers of two of our best employees. We have to swear to the utmost secrecy."

Everyone in the group nodded in agreement.

"We'll keep this information a secret. Both candidates are excellent choices," Hannah O'Sullivan said as she adjusted her glasses. Hannah was one of the bank's wealthiest investors, and having her support would help sway the others to his eventual choice to temporarily take over the reins. "However, there's an army of reporters outside and bank clients are worried sick."

"We've come up with a PR strategy," Kirk reminded her.

"That's all very well and good." Her lips formed a thin line. "But we still don't know why your parents were arrested. It's a miracle that SIB stocks haven't crashed. If it weren't for your cousin Ian here, and his tireless work this past week, stock prices might have been wiped out entirely. Some of the panic could have been avoided if you had gone on TV and tried to calm everyone down. Instead, you've come to work for a handful of hours and have been running the show by email and through your assistant. Is there something you're trying to keep from us?"

He suppressed a sigh. "I had to keep my attention on other, more important, matters."

Hannah's eyes narrowed. "What could be more important than your father's empire?"

Bethany was more important. For years he had dreamed of taking over the bank from his father. Planned and plotted to get what he knew was rightfully his. And while he still wanted to be in charge, Bethany made that original dream pale in comparison to his desire to see her safe. Nothing mattered without her in his life.

Hannah must have seen the expression on his face change, because her frown deepened. "It isn't a what... it's a who." She leaned forward conspiratorially. "There's been some gossip going around about you, Kirk. Please, tell me it's just idle rumor."

His stomach tightened. The reporter who had been caught trespassing had probably sent the rumor mill into overdrive after he'd been tossed off his property. Though the reporter hadn't seen Bethany at his mansion, somehow he had known she was there.

It was then that he remembered that Bethany had suspected her own mother of leaking the truth to make some quick money from the press. Maybe her mother was still talking to the media. Elle Livingston seemed bitter and resentful enough to betray her own daughter if she thought it would ruin a Sterling in the process.

"What kind of gossip?" he demanded.

"I hate repeating it..." Hannah let out a frustrated sigh, the lines on her face more pronounced. Clearly the stress of the past several days was getting to her. She had invested too much money in SIB to want to let this go. "A few days ago, I heard that a member of the Livingston family was seen on your property. At first I thought it was nonsense, but I've heard from several trusted sources that you were seen at a public event with this Livingston woman."

He scowled. "We were seen together. So what?"

"My source says that you were in the same room as a Livingston and that everything went much smoother than expected—"

"What exactly do you expect me to have done? Make a scene at a charity event?" he pressed. "And who is your source?"

"A government official who must remain anonymous," Hannah said quickly.

From the way her tone sharpened, that government official was someone high up. Maybe it was the mayor. Or worse, maybe it was the city's former police chief. Who still hadn't been located. The chance that Hannah O'Sullivan might be in contact with Damien Kemp set him on edge. Kemp could very well have been Bethany's attacker, and wondering if Hannah was on his side was unnerving.

"Why do you get to keep your friend's anonymity while I have to tell you the details of my private life?" he asked.

"Your parents were arrested on the same day as Lloyd Livingston," Hannah reminded him. "They're obviously all involved in the same alleged crime, even if we don't know what the charges are yet. Now there are wild rumors about you and Lloyd Livingston's daughter. It doesn't look good for the bank, Kirk. It looks like some kind of conspiracy is going on—"

"That's ridiculous," he said, cutting her off. "You know me. Do you actually think I'm some kind of crook? Do you think I'm in on some plot with Lloyd Livingston's daughter?"

"I'm not telling you what *I* think," Hannah snapped. "I'm telling you what the media and the public will think in light of your parents' arrest. In light of Livingston's scandal from ten years ago. We're in a precarious position, and your usual arrogance is going to cost us."

"Livingston's daughter isn't involved with any of this, so leave her out of it," he said firmly. "She has nothing to do with the bank or anything else—"

A knock on the conference room door cut him short.

"Come in," Hannah said sharply.

His assistant Camille poked her head in and grimaced. "Sorry to bother you, Mr. Sterling, but you have a visitor. She says it's urgent."

"She's going to have to wait," he said.

Camille's eyes darted around as if she was too anxious to reveal more. "Sir, it's... Ms. Walker. She's right outside."

At the mention of Bethany, he glanced out the glass window and spotted her on the opposite end of the floor. Bethany was standing next to Jane Tanner, the wealthy heiress who was investing in her shop.

His heart sank. It wasn't his usual reaction to seeing Bethany, but after he had just tried to protect her seeing her now was going to make things worse.

Hannah gazed out the window and gasped. "Good Lord. There's Livingston's daughter right now." She turned back to him and her glacial blue eyes narrowed. "What was it you were saying? Livingston's daughter has nothing to do with the bank? If she has nothing to do with the bank, why is she standing right outside?"

"THIS IS SO EXCITING," Jane practically squealed.

Bethany linked her arm with Jane's, suddenly overcome with happy anticipation. A thrill jolted through her. Bethany could hardly believe that it was finally happening. Her dream was coming true and she couldn't wait to share the news with Kirk.

"I can't wait to tell him the good news," Bethany said as she saw him step out of one of the bank's glass-encased meeting rooms.

Getting an early-morning call from the real estate agent who had been helping them had been an unexpected surprise. The moment she got Jane up to speed on the good news, Jane had offered to pick her up and head to SIB to finalize everything.

There had been a crowd of reporters outside, but luckily for them they had managed to sneak in through a bank entrance that VIP clients like Jane had access to.

Bethany's excitement turned to apprehension as Kirk approached them, the expression on his face grim. When they greeted him, the look on his face didn't change.

"Is everything okay?" she asked him. "Oh, gosh, we've interrupted something important, haven't we?"

"We can talk in my office," he said.

Minutes later, they were settling into the comfortable chairs in the corner of his huge office. His assistant walked in, set down three cups of steaming coffee, and slipped back out again.

"We're so sorry to come down here on such short notice," Jane said. "But we've just gotten the best news ever." Jane paused for effect.

"You're not going to leave me in suspense, are you?" Kirk asked.

Jane was giddy with excitement as she fidgeted in her chair. "Oh, you tell him, Bethany."

"The owner of the commercial property we chose is going to rent the place to us," Bethany said.

Suddenly the grim expression that he'd had on his face since she had spotted him vanished, and he smiled. "Are you serious? Which property is it? When are you going to open the place?"

"The same property that you saw when you dropped by to visit me," she said.

The shop was in the perfect place. An upscale mall that got a good amount of traffic.

"I remember," he said with a nod. "That was a great location. So the owner agreed to rent it?"

She nodded. "Yes. Originally he wanted to sell the place, but Jane finally convinced him to rent it to us at a great price. Earlier this morning he told our real estate agent that he had changed his mind about selling and was willing to rent it to us." Her entire body was flooded with excitement. Finally, she was going to have a space for her very own shop. After so much recent trauma, something wonderful was going to happen. She couldn't wait to get to work.

"Well, if you'd both like to sign off on paying the first month's rent, I can get the contract right now," he said.

"That's why we dropped by," Jane said. "Bethany wanted us to call you first, but I thought what the hell, let's surprise Kirk with the good news."

He smiled a smile that didn't reach his eyes. "It definitely is a surprise. Let me go get the contract for you to sign."

As he stood up to head over to his desk, her heart squeezed. Something was definitely wrong. It was probably work-related. From all the reporters who were gathered outside, SIB was definitely going through its share of difficulties.

He brought over some documents that Bethany and Jane quickly signed.

"Now, I'm going to wire the first month's rent to the owner," Jane said. "After that, we have even more work to do."

With the shop almost rented, their hard work really had only just started. "We're going to need to start working on furnishing the place and interviewing potential employees," Bethany said.

Jane stood up. "Right. We can schedule a meeting for next week so we can go over the next few steps. In the meantime, why don't I leave you two celebrate alone?" Jane gave her a meaningful look and grinned. Though Bethany hadn't actually told Jane that she and Kirk were dating, Jane seemed to have figured that out on her own.

With a final wave goodbye Jane walked out of the office, leaving Bethany alone with Kirk.

"Is everything okay?" she asked him. "If you're worried that those reporters might have seen us, don't be. Jane and I took the VIP entrance."

He leaned back in his chair and forced out a sigh. "The problem is that some of the shareholders and senior executives I was having a meeting with saw you."

She bit her lip. "Is that a problem? I'm so sorry, I let my excitement get the best of me. I should have called before I stopped by."

"It isn't your fault." He reached across the low table and took her hands. "I just have to find a way to calm the senior executives down. They suspect that we're together."

Swallowing hard, she pulled away from him to pick up her cup of coffee. "And that looks bad because of my father's time in prison and his arrest."

"That's how they think the public and the media will see it," he murmured. "I don't think the senior staff has a real opinion one way or the other. They're just worried that the media might run with the story of you and me being together. Then they could spin things to look make it look like we're in on some kind of conspiracy with our parents."

Her eyes widened before she took a sip of coffee to calm her nerves. "That's crazy."

"That's what I thought, but try to imagine how this would look to people who don't know us," he said. "Our families have been tangled up for years now. First my parents worked for your father, and then reaped the benefits of his downfall. A downfall they had a hand in. Now, ten years later, they all get arrested and their kids are dating each other?"

"The media is going to love this," she said miserably. "I can't afford bad press if I want to open the shop."

"I know that," he said gently. "We still have to prepare for the worst. We'll do everything to stay out of the public eye until our parents' legal issues are settled."

"What do we do if the press does run with this story?" she asked.

He ran a hand through his hair. "We'll have to spin things in our favor. I do have an idea, though."

She leaned forward. "You have an idea? What is it?"

"Yes, I do." Kirk clenched his jaw, his change in demeanor putting her on edge. "But you're really not going to like it."

Chapter 9

It was rare for her to dread knowing what Kirk was thinking. Right now her stomach was in knots and her nerves were frayed.

Bethany gazed across the table at him and noticed the way his green eyes darkened. A cold, foreboding air seemed to radiate from him and she shivered. He was right. She really wasn't going to like this. Straightening her spine and throwing her shoulders back, she said, "You can tell me your idea."

"We need to get some positive stories out to the press," he began. "Show them that you aren't what the press tried to portray you as when your dad was first arrested."

After her father was arrested the first time, the media had insinuated that she had known about his alleged crimes. They had painted her as a spoiled rich girl who had helped her father cover up his supposed misdeeds. Some of the worst gossip rags had speculated that she had spent her father's ill-gotten money on fancy clothes and cars. When she had taken out a student loan to get into college reporters had lied, accusing her of using stolen money to buy her way in.

"They think I'm a thief. Just like they think my father is," she said.

"You were also arrested a while back," he reminded her with a grimace.

There hadn't been any charges, but with her family's history that wouldn't matter. The reporter who had trespassed on Kirk's property a few days ago would be nothing compared to what the media would do when they had her in their sights again.

"So, what could be so bad about using a positive story?" she asked, puzzled.

"I was thinking we could release a few stories about how you got all that money back from Damien Kemp and set up a foundation for your father's victims."

Indignation flooded her and she held up her hands. "What? No way. Absolutely not."

"Bethany, we have to do something to push back against these rumors," he insisted.

"I'm not going to throw those poor people under the bus to drum up some good press. Can you imagine how awful it will be for them when they realize I'm the one who set up the fund for them?" Even though she still had no memory of her attack, she remembered everything about the auction the day before. They had figured out how the city's police chief had been laundering money and pressuring their parents to do shady things they still didn't know about.

Taking that ill-gotten money from a slimy crook like Damien Kemp had been one of the best decisions she'd ever made. Especially since she had insisted that they set up a foundation to help the people who had lost everything because of her father's alleged crimes.

"Look, it's either a positive story or one that makes people feel sorry for you," he said. "And there's no way in hell I'm going to use the trauma of your attack for any reason, so the foundation is the only option."

Her chest tightened as anxiety took hold. "I can't believe I'm hearing this. I'm not going to use this story to save a bank that my family doesn't even own anymore."

"If you're not going to do it for the bank then do it for yourself," he said. "Do it for your career."

She gasped. "What—"

"Your shop is going to open soon." The darkness in his eyes vanished, and concern flashed in their depths. "When you announce the grand opening, what do you think the press will try to do? Even if they don't have a negative story ready to print, they'll still try to use your past against you."

Her heart fell. Ice-cold dread slipped down her spine. For one wonderful moment she'd had her dreams in the palm of her hand. But now...

All her hard work. The years of sacrifice. Slaving away over sewing machines to make costumes for theater productions nobody ever saw. Searching desperately for clients. Taking on a mountain of debt she still hadn't paid off. It was all going to blow up in her face because of what her father might have done.

Suddenly her temples started to throb. The new scar in her forehead began to pulse with pain. The office started to spin and she gripped the arm of the chair.

"Bethany." Kirk was by her side in an instant, taking her hands in his. "Can you hear me? Are you okay?"

She squeezed her eyes shut, desperate for the pain to end. "My head. It hurts."

"Dammit! What have I done? I pushed you too hard." The anguish in his voice made her tremble. The last thing she wanted to do was scare him.

Bethany opened her eyes. "I feel dizzy."

"I'm taking you back to the hospital," he said firmly.

"No, it's okay. I just need a minute."

"I'm not taking any chances with a head injury." He wrapped a strong arm around her shoulders and helped her to her feet. "Don't worry about the money. I'll take care of it."

She opened her mouth to protest, but quickly closed it when he gave her a hard stare.

"No arguments." He guided her across the office and opened the door to walk her out.

They took the VIP entrance to get to his car and Kirk helped her into the passenger seat. Her hands shot out as intense pain needled through the back of her head. Needing to steady herself, she reached for the dashboard. More pain. And then everything went black.

THE BEAM OF LIGHT SHINING in her eyes nearly blinded her. She snapped her eyes closed.

"I'm going to need you to open your eyes, Ms. Walker."

That familiar voice.

"Dr. Stavropoulos?" She forced her eyes open, blinking rapidly to adjust to the bright light. "What's happening?"

"Oh, dear. I think you blacked out again."

Again? She swallowed hard. "What? I...I blacked out in the car." With a groan she sat up straight, realizing that she was on an examining table in a doctor's office.

The doctor took a step back. "You did. But you regained consciousness quickly and Mr. Sterling brought you to my office. You were conscious when you came in, but I think you blacked out again for a moment. That's probably why you're confused."

"My head feels fuzzy," she murmured.

"Do you remember coming into my office?" Dr. Stavropoulos asked.

Bethany forced herself to think. She remembered getting into Kirk's car. Images of the ride to the hospital flashed in her mind. A reassuring warmth spread across her and she realized that she could remember Kirk holding her hand tightly as he led her to the doctor's office. The memory of it nearly brought tears to her eyes. After dealing with the indifference from her own family, having someone as concerned and wonderful as Kirk watching over her nearly moved her to tears.

"Where is he?" she asked. "Where's Kirk?"

"He's right outside," Dr. Stavropoulos replied. "Waiting anxiously to see how you're doing."

"Am I okay?" she asked.

"Why don't you lie back for a minute so that I can take a look at your eyes," the doctor suggested in a soothing tone.

She did as he told her and Dr. Stavropoulos looked her over. When he was finished he set his instruments aside.

"Is everything okay?" she asked in a shaky voice.

"You seem to be dealing with post-concussion syndrome," he explained.

"Is that bad?"

"If we manage it correctly, you'll have a full recovery," the doctor replied. "It isn't uncommon for people who have suffered head injuries to deal with post-concussion issues. At times it's something specific that triggers it."

"Like what?" She chewed her lip.

"Anything from anxiety to stress can set it off," he said.

"Oh."

The doctor titled his head and studied her. "Have you had any reason to be anxious or stressed recently, Ms. Walker?"

"Well, I was attacked," she said. "And I still can't remember it, which is a bit scary. My dad is going through some real trouble right now. Plus, there's all this stuff going on with my career."

Realizing how hungry the media was for a scandal had terrified her. All the happiness over getting a shop location had vanished when she finally understood that the press wasn't going to relent. Wasn't going to leave her in peace while she focused on work.

"Sounds like you've got a lot on your plate. That kind of stress could have something to do with it." A pensive expression settled on the doctor's face. "You know we've focused a lot on your physical recovery, but you might need to focus on your mental health as well. After a traumatic experience like the one you've had, it might be a good idea to talk to a therapist. Even if you don't remember you experience yet, it can be helpful to talk things out with a professional."

Dr. Stavropoulos scheduled another appointment and then gave her details on therapists he recommended. With the visit over, he walked her to his office door and opened it to let her out.

Kirk was pacing in the hall right outside. He stopped in his tracks the second he spotted her and rushed over to her. "Is everything okay?"

"She just needs to avoid stress for the next couple of days," the doctor said. "Ms. Walker, you should focus on taking care of yourself. Try to slow down a little."

"'I'm going to try," she promised. "It's just that there are so many things out of my control."

"I understand," Dr. Stavropoulos said. "What you can try to do is come up with a plan with the therapist you choose. Remember to take a little quiet time for yourself, and remember to breathe when things get overwhelming." He said his goodbyes and headed down the hall.

"You don't have to stay in the hospital?" Kirk asked.

She shook her head. "The doctor says I have post-concussion syndrome, so I need to de-stress. He also suggested I talk to a therapist about the things that have been stressing me out lately."

He lifted his hands to cup her face. The sensation of his touch warmed her heart. Reminded her that, for the first time in years, she had someone she could lean on. And count on.

"I did this." A dark shadow darkened his eyes, and suddenly he looked haunted. The raw devastation she saw on his face was a crushing weight on her shoulders. "This is my fault. If I hadn't pushed you so hard..." He turned from her and sighed heavily. "You were so excited about your shop and I ruined your moment so much that you ended up in the hospital again."

The anguish in his voice tore her to pieces. How could he blame himself for what her attacker had caused? "None of this is your fault." She placed her hand on his shoulder. "You didn't hurt me."

Turning around to face her again, Kirk took her hand. "I don't want to cause you any more stress."

"You haven't," she assured him.

"You passed out right outside the bank," he said. "Instead of celebrating your success or checking to see how you were doing, I suggested something I shouldn't have."

She slipped her hand away to wrap her arms around him. The strength of his hard body made her feel so safe. No matter how scared she was about her attack, she knew that Kirk's strength would make her strong, too. "That doesn't make this your fault. Besides, I think we've both been stressed lately."

"Our parents getting arrested hasn't helped things. Which is why we have to fight to help them get out on bail and come home." He wrapped his powerful arms around her and held her in place against him. Even through all the layers of his clothing she could feel the muscles beneath. The ripple of power that simmered just below the surface. Only Kirk's strength could ease her anxiety about being in a hospital.

Needing to feel the weight of his lips on hers, she stood on her toes to kiss him. Warmth spiraled through her at the delicious contact. He returned the kiss, prying her lips apart with this tongue. Sparks of desire turned her all hot and breathless in his arms. His tongue swirled as he expertly explored her mouth. A low, satisfied groan escaped his throat, his grip on her tightening. Their bodies were pressed so close together now, Bethany could swear she felt the rhythm of his heartbeat. They were that connected to each other. That much a part of each other now.

He pulled back reluctantly to rest his forehead on hers. "I'm sorry about pushing you to reveal the truth about the foundation. I didn't have the right to ask you to make that call."

"You only suggested I go to the media with a positive story because you want to protect me. I get that," she said softly. "My shop is going to open soon, and I do need a PR strategy to have the best opening possible. I was so concerned about getting investment money that I didn't think too much about how the media would treat me. You reminded me of that."

"We'll come up with a strategy that you're comfortable with," he assured her. "No matter what you decide, I'm proud of you, Bethany. Your shop is going to be amazing, and when you're feeling better we should celebrate your success."

His words touched her heart and she smiled. "I can't wait to celebrate with you."

Kirk wrapped a heavy arm around her shoulders. "In the meantime, let's get you home so that you can rest like the doctor ordered."

She walked with him through the hospital, grateful that she didn't have to spend the night again. Thank goodness Kirk had ignored her protests and taken her to the hospital. Otherwise things might have been much worse. Just like he had on the day he had found her in the kitchen and rescued her, Kirk had saved her once again. The fact that her attacker was still out there frightened her, but she knew that as long as Kirk was with her she would be safe.

SEVERAL DAYS LATER Kirk decided to spend the day working from home. The board at Sterling Investment Bank was still deliberating over his two choices to take temporary control of the bank. Pressure was on them to act quickly. They had no idea if, or when, his parents would be released from jail, and the longer the bank went without stability the worse it would get with the media. Keeping that uncertainty out of the media spotlight was top priority.

So, while the board debated, he could spend the day video-conferencing investors to reassure them. Investors were anxious about the bank's future with its president still in jail, so he had to be ready to convince them that everything was under control. No matter how out of control life seemed right now, it was his job to exude confidence.

By mid-morning he had talked to enough investors to have earned a break, so he stepped out of his home study and headed into the living room.

The dining table was set up buffet-style like he had requested. He poured himself some coffee and took a seat to check his phone messages. One message from his assistant caught his eye. A link to a newspaper story. Hitting the link took him to a story about SIB. His eyebrows shot up when he read the headline. Sweat formed on his brow as he realized that the story he had been trying to keep under wraps had made the national news.

Chapter 10

"How could they have found out about this?" he barked into his cell phone.

"Look, I don't know. I've been trying to help your parents out of jail, so I haven't had the time to leak anything. I swear it wasn't me," his cousin Ian replied on the other end. "Someone else must have leaked it."

Kirk stepped into this study and shut the door. "Who? Everyone at that meeting swore they wouldn't say anything. Nobody was supposed to know that someone was taking over for my father until we announced it. Now a national newspaper has gotten the story and they've even leaked the names of the two candidates."

"Kirk, the truth was going to come out eventually. It's not some scandalous secret. How bad could it be if the press leaks the news a few days or weeks before we announce?" Ian asked.

"It's bad because a national newspaper has gotten wind of it. This isn't local news anymore. The national news has not only leaked SIB's plans, but they've also put my parents on the front page of every newspaper in the country. The only reason SIB has weathered so much bad press is because it's been local. How the hell will our shares stay steady if the whole country has its eye on us?" Kirk thundered. "It was bad enough when local reporters tried to break into my house—"

"Someone tried to break in?" Ian asked in shock.

"They literally scaled the wall of my property," Kirk said through clenched teeth. "We'll never get any peace now. I'm going to have to triple the security. And the worst thing is that this is going to turn into a circus. The media will probably camp outside the jail my parents are locked up in, or they'll start digging through our private lives."

"They'll dig through Bethany's, too," Ian warned.

Bethany. He hadn't spoken to her all morning because, for the last couple of days, she had slept in. When she eventually woke up he was going to have to tell her about the leak. With the national media speculating on SIB's future, keeping the truth from her wasn't an option. "Breaking the news to her is going to stress her out even more." Kirk blew out a breath. "With her dad in jail again, media attention is going to be worse than what she dealt with as a kid."

"It's either you tell her or she finds out from the news," Ian said. "From what you've told me about her, media attention during her father's first arrest was traumatic for her. If she needs to prepare for more scrutiny, it's better that she hears it from you."

The stress was only going to make things worse for her. She had seemed to be getting stronger and healthier over the past few days. Now he was going to have to tell her about this new crisis.

He ran his hand through his hair in frustration. "We have to figure out who leaked the information."

"I have to take a phone call from your dad's lawyer soon, but afterwards I can quietly question everyone who was at the meeting," Ian suggested. "They're more likely to tell me the truth. You're their boss, so they won't want to reveal anything."

"Does my dad's lawyer think he can get them out of jail?" Kirk hoped his cousin could give him some good news.

"He sounded optimistic in his last email, but I don't want to get anyone's hopes up until we hear from the judge deciding on bail. I'll focus on talking to the lawyer and questioning everyone about the leak."

"Thanks, Ian. While you do that I'll get information from my contacts in the media," Kirk said. "Somebody has to know where the leak came from."

"No problem. You go break the news to Bethany. I'll be in touch after I question everyone," Ian said and then hung up.

Kirk sighed and headed for the door of his study. He opened it, and found Bethany standing outside with her hand raised to knock on the door.

"Kirk, have you watched the news today?" she asked, her voice tinged with worry.

His heart sank. She had already found out about the leak. Which meant he hadn't been around to soften the blow for her. "My assistant sent me the news."

"But didn't you want me to keep the news about the temporary president a secret?" she asked.

"We can talk over breakfast." He placed a firm hand on the small of her back and started to guide her to the dining room. If he could get her to sit down and eat something, maybe that might make the mounting stress easier on her.

When they got to the dining room, he pulled out a chair for her and then sat on the opposite side of the table. "Are you hungry?" He poured some freshly squeezed orange juice and slid the glass over to her.

She pursed her full lips. "Why do I get the feeling you're stalling?"

"Obviously you know that the names of the two candidates for the bank's temporary president have been leaked."

"I saw it on one of the cable news channels," she explained. "Isn't the national news leaking the story a bad thing?"

He grimaced and pushed his hair out of his eyes. "It might not be that bad."

"You don't have to sugarcoat this for me." She reached for a plate and put a croissant on it.

"You're dealing with a lot of stress right now," he said. "If I add to that you might end up back in the hospital."

"Kirk, if you don't tell me what you're thinking I'll go crazy with worry. That's way worse than just laying out the truth."

"Okay." He took a deep breath. "I was just on the phone with Ian. He's going to try to find out where this leak came from."

"I promise I didn't leak this news," she said.

He balked. "Bethany, I swear I'm not accusing you. That hadn't even crossed my mind."

She held up her hand. "Our relationship didn't exactly start honestly, so I wouldn't blame you for being suspicious."

"I wasn't suspicious," he insisted. "You didn't leak this. I trust you, okay?"

"Okay. So, you didn't leak this and neither did I." She chewed on her lower lip as she started to think. There was something so endearing about her when she got lost in thought like this. Her nose scrunched up as she chewed her lip, totally oblivious as to how beautiful she looked right now. Her golden hair was damp around her shoulders, and the scent of her flowery shampoo filled the air.

No matter how stressful things got, he would always ache to touch her. To have her soft skin underneath his fingertips. To run his hand through her hair and wrap it around his hand so that he could kiss her.

There was a sweetness about the way she wanted to help him. She had a kind heart. Much kinder than he deserved after he failed to protect her.

"Who stands to benefit from a leak like this?" she asked.

He shrugged. "Someone who hates the two candidates."

"Or someone who wants to see the bank fail," she said.

Apprehension settled in his gut and he grabbed his phone out of his pocket. "That makes way more sense than my theory." He scrolled through his messages again.

Panicked messages from his assistant. Company shares were dropping because of the news. The uncertainty was dragging SIB shares down. News about a temporary president in the aftermath of his father's arrest was probably scaring the hell out of the markets. His cell phone started to ring. Which was never a good sign because his assistant dealt with the majority of his business calls.

"Is that work?" she asked, glancing at this phone.

He declined the call with a frown. "It's one of SIB's shareholders." Dealing with a shareholder's panic right now would make him second-guess himself. They couldn't afford him to be anything less than confident about the decisions he made in the next seventy-two hours. "I can't talk to them right now. The most important thing I can do is track down who leaked the information and make sure they don't leak anything else."

She started eating her croissant. "If it's someone who wants to see the bank fail, do you think that could help you narrow things down?"

"There's got to be a reason they'd want the bank to fail, though," he murmured.

"But who would gain from a struggling bank?"

"Someone who might be able to make money from it," he said.

Her eyes widened in surprise. "What? You think someone is trying to make a profit from all this?"

"After all the things we've learned about the shadiness going on at SIB, that wouldn't surprise me," he said. "Damien Kemp is still out there. I've been in touch with my lawyer to see if he's found out Kemp's whereabouts, and so far there's nothing. It's like Kemp disappeared without a trace."

"But if he's out of town how could he have linked information he didn't even have?"

"That's what I'm still trying to figure out." He drummed his fingers on the table, lost in thought. "If this information leaked because Kemp's bosses wanted to make a profit, they'd buy SIB's shares. Right now, the price of those shares is falling. So, if they buy the shares when they're cheap, they could be sold at a later date at record profits. That's if things bounce back."

"Of course things will bounce back," she said confidently. "You're the one who hunted down Damien Kemp even though your father warned you how dangerous he was. I've seen what you can do, Kirk. SIB is lucky to have you."

Her belief in him seemed to be endless. Somehow he was going to make sure he proved her right. He had to solve this. Figure out who was still trying to control his parents' empire, and bring them down once and for all.

Kirk paused to go over everything in his mind. "So, the theory is that some shady characters out there are counting on me to save the bank after this crisis so that they can make a killing in profits." His body went rigid at the thought of someone rigging the system like this.

"We have to find whoever leaked the story," she said. "It wouldn't be right to let someone make money from a financial crisis they created in the first place."

Dread overtook him. He had no way of knowing if his theory was correct right now, but a terrible thought dawned on him. One he hadn't even considered. "It's more than that, Bethany. They won't only make a huge profit. If whoever did this buys enough shares, they could own a large percentage of the bank and push my family out for good."

SHOCK AT HIS WORDS made her go still. "What are you saying? That you and your family could lose the bank?" Her heart started to race at the thought of Kirk losing everything he had worked so hard to achieve. He'd started off dirt-poor and ended up going to business school. Then he'd fought his way to his position as vice president. She had never known anyone who had worked as hard as he had.

"It's just a theory, but I think that's a real possibility based on what's been going on," he said grimly. "We need more proof."

She pushed her plate away, her appetite long gone now. "We get proof by finding out who leaked the news to the media."

He nodded. "Yes, that's right. The leaker has to be working with Damien Kemp. His reach probably goes beyond the police force."

"Do you think the leak is connected to our parents getting arrested? Or maybe my attack?" A shudder ran through her. Not being able to remember what had happened was so unsettling it was starting to make her sick.

"I'm going to call my security company and tell them to increase security at the mansion." He grabbed his phone again and dialed a number. "There are way too many dangerous people plotting against us. Give me a minute." Kirk got to his feet and pressed the phone up to his ear.

He started talking to the person on the other end in a low voice that frightened her. Not because Kirk frightened her, but because she could hear from his tone that he was taking this very seriously.

Anxiety tugged painfully at her stomach. Now, on top of worrying about Damien Kemp and her unknown attacker, she had to worry about some other shadowy figure that was trying to ruin them.

Months ago, news about Kirk Sterling potentially losing the bank and his fortune would have filled her with glee. But that was before she had grown to care for him. Now, she wanted Kirk to succeed with all her heart. To take over the bank that had originally belonged to her father.

That thought shocked her. Because it was the first time she had truly sided with Kirk. For most of the time she had known Kirk she had balanced her feelings. She had felt equal concern for her family's fate as she had for Kirk's. Yet now she wanted Kirk to succeed. Wanted him to fulfill his dreams and take his place as the bank's president. His rightful place.

Out of all the people who had tried to lead the bank, only Kirk had shown that he was worthy. Her own father had worked with criminals to get ahead. Kirk's parents had put up with money laundering. Meanwhile, Kirk had refused to do either of those things even though it would have been easier for him.

"There's going to be an increase in security personnel," he said, pulling her from the haze of her thoughts. He put his phone back into his pocket and focused his attention on her. "I'm going to make sure there's a guard just for the guesthouse."

She swallowed hard and nodded. "Thank you. Is there anything I can help with?"

Without a word, he approached her and placed a firm hand on her shoulder. "This isn't a problem that you need to solve, Bethany."

"I know, but—"

She fell silent as his hand drifted down and he dragged his thumb across her lips. Heat bloomed inside her. Just his touch alone could get her to do anything. And that, along with the realization that she now wanted to him to run the bank, sent a shiver through her entire body. This was bigger than a relationship. Now, she was his. Completely and totally. She would be loyal to him for the rest of her life.

His eyes held hers for a long moment. Like he wanted to say something important, but didn't know if now was the right time. Finally, he said, "Don't you have an appointment with your therapist today?"

"I...I do," she stammered. The warmth that had bloomed inside her turned to an unbearable heat. She was burning hotter than any flame. It was in that split second that she knew that flame would only ever burn for him.

If for some reason he lost his fortune now, she would never leave his side. She was his until the very end.

"My chauffer will take you to your appointment," he said in a firm tone. "One of the guards will escort you as well. I'm not taking any chances."

"What about you? Will you try to talk to senior staff at the bank?"

He nodded. "I've got a ton of conference calls to make to deal with the leak. On top of all that I'm going to be calling every single newspaper and magazine editor I've ever come in contact with. Someone has to know who told the press about this. If I figure that out, I can stop the people who have been coming after my family for all these years."

Her insides quivered with anxiety, but she found the strength to stand up. "Promise you'll tell me the minute you get any more clues or information."

Kirk leaned towards her and captured her lips in a tender kiss. "I promise. Now go get ready. Your doctor gave very clear instructions and I expect you to follow them."

It was hard to argue with him when he got bossy like this. And why would she want to? Kirk taking charge thrilled her as much as it drove her crazy.

She pressed a final kiss to his lips and turned around to slip away. Since her attack, her relationship with him had deepened. Grown more intense. So intense that it was like they had moved into a whole new phase of their relationship. He had seen her at her most vulnerable. Probably even saved her life. Now he was fighting to save not only her, but his empire and his family as well. The strength in him was changing her. Making her stronger, too.

That strength was so important, now more than ever. With a new enemy out there, she was going to need to be stronger than she had ever been before.

Chapter 11

"Kirk, you home?" she called as she headed up the winding staircase.

She had just come back from her therapy session, but Kirk was nowhere to be found. He wasn't in his study like she had expected and he wasn't anywhere downstairs. None of the staff seemed to know where he was either.

Heart pounding, she rushed into his bedroom. He wasn't here.

The sound of running water sent a twinge of apprehension through her body. "Kirk?"

"I'm in here!"

Relief washed over her, and she followed the sound of his voice into the luxurious bathroom that was adjacent to his room.

She gasped when she stepped into the bathroom. There were bright red rose petals strewn across the marble floor. Steam was rising from the enormous bathtub and the scent of roses filled the air.

In the middle of it all was Kirk, putting his hand underneath the water faucet to test the temperature of the water as it filled the tub.

He turned to look at her and smiled. "How was your therapy session?"

"It went surprisingly well. Talking things out helped to take some of the pressure off." She peered at the water in the tub, noting the red rose petals that floated amid all the suds.

"Since today has been so stressful, I thought of a way to help you relax," he said. "The doctor wanted you to de-stress, so I figured you could take a nice long bath."

"The water is still warm. How did you know I was here?" she asked.

"Your bodyguard called to let me know you were home," he answered.

"Oh." She didn't know if she liked the idea of a security detail that watched her every move. No amount of time was going to get her to adjust to it, though she understood why Kirk was so concerned about her safety. "This is so wonderful, Kirk. Thank you."

"You can get in and I'll leave you to it." As he stepped away, she reached for his arm to stop him.

"You don't have to leave," she said in a low tone.

The steam in the bathroom was so luxurious and warm that she was more than ready to peel off her clothes. She reached for the hem of her dress and pulled it off. "Why don't you join me?" she asked in a husky voice.

Steam caressed her exposed skin as his hungry eyes raked over her body. She didn't know which was more exquisite—the sensation of the perfumed steam enveloping her, or the burning intensity of his possessive gaze.

A wicked smile played on his lips as he approached her. Kirk's large hands lowered to grasp her waist. Despite the heat rising in the bathroom, she shivered underneath his fingertips. The last few days had been stressful, and taking the time to enjoy his company would more than make up for it.

With a glint in his green eyes, he reached behind her to unhook her lacy bra. His hands roamed to her exposed breasts and he stroked her sensitive nipples with this thumbs. Desire left her gasping for breath. A soft moan nearly escaped her throat, but the sound died when he captured her lips with his in a searing kiss that melted her thoughts away.

His demanding mouth crushed her lips against his. Her body's response to him was instantaneous. Liquid heat pooled between her thighs.

She parted her lips, inviting him in. Their tongues met. Entwined. Slowly, achingly slowly, she was coming undone as his perfect mouth sent sparks through her. The kiss was greedy but lingering. Kirk took his time to devour her, pulling her body to his as he deepened the kiss.

The sensation of her exposed breasts crushed against his hard chest sent a thrill through her. It was like her body was made for his. As his tongue swept into her mouth, the most secret part of her throbbed with an aching, indescribable need. She might have melted in his arms if he didn't tear his mouth from hers to stare deep into her eyes.

"You get into the tub and wait for me." He slid his hands away from her to unbutton his shirt.

Her pulse quickened, thrilled at the prospect of him getting into the warm water with her. Hands shaky with excitement, she reached down to peel off her panties before walking over to the bathtub. The aromatic steam beckoned to her and she dipped her foot into the water to test it. Perfect. Warmth rippled across her skin and she climbed into the tub.

Foamy water swirled around her, heating her skin. She let out a satisfied sigh as the remainder of her stress seemed to just evaporate.

"Bethany."

The sound of her name in his low baritone forced her to look up at him. The way he said her name was filled with a raw desire that made her tremble.

He peeled off the rest of his clothes, leaving him completely naked. His rock-hard body looked like it was made of sculptured marble. Kirk was masculine perfection, from his chiseled features to his broad shoulders, all the way down his muscular torso, and lower still.

His erection was huge. The sight of it made her lick her lips.

"Bethany, if you could see how beautiful you look..." His voice trailed off as he stopped to gaze at her, pure lust burning in the depths of his green eyes. Without saying anything else, he got into the tub behind her. She scooted over to give his huge body some room. The weight of it sent the warm water splashing up around her breasts.

Suddenly, she felt his powerful arm around her as he pulled her against his chest. His large hand rested on her stomach, his touch firm and possessive. Sighing happily she leaned back, resting her head against his chest, his body anchoring her as she enjoyed the warmth of the water.

"You know," he whispered against her ear, "we can't have sex."

"What? Why not?"

He chuckled. "You're eager, aren't you?" Kirk paused. "Today has been taken a toll. I could hear it in your voice when you came into my bedroom. Any kind of rigorous activity might be too much for you today."

"Oh." She pouted, unable to hide her disappointment.

"But that doesn't mean I can't help you enjoy yourself." He nibbled at her ear, his hand wandering down to the juncture of her thighs.

"*Ohhhhh.*" Sparks of pleasure shook her body.

"Do you want me to keep going?" he whispered.

With a whimper she pleaded, "Yes. Don't stop."

A wicked laugh rumbled in his chest.

His hand was still on her and he teased her, sliding his finger into her.

Bliss made her body jerk and she started to shudder against him. Suddenly, the heat of his sensuous mouth brushed against her shoulder, making her quiver as he started to expertly stroke her with his finger.

Each stroke was seductive torment. Sliding his finger in and out of her created the most delicious friction she had ever experienced in her life. As she moaned his name she clamped down around him, greedy to have him inside her for eternity.

As if he could sense her excitement he eased another finger into her slippery depths, sending another wave of pleasure crashing through her.

Her heart started to race as the pleasure intensified. She was being overtaken by the most incredible sensations. Here she was, held against his body, being caressed by fragrant steam while he gave her more bliss than she'd ever felt in her life. Every worry in her head vanished. Right now she was nothing but pure feeling.

"Oh, damn." Needing to steady herself against the onslaught of so much bliss, she gripped the side of the tub and moaned.

While he worked her sex with his fingers he kept his lips on her, kissing a trail up her neck. Ecstasy filled her, making her pant desperately.

The pace of his strokes increased as he stroked her with a rhythm that seemed to match her own heartbeat perfectly. Pleasure mounted until she was on the edge of blissful release. She quivered against him, her breathless moans getting louder and louder. Suddenly her climax jolted through her so hard and fast that she saw stars as she came.

She fell back against him, gasping for air in the aftermath of her orgasm. "I never want to get out of this tub," she said with a breathy laugh.

"Good," he murmured against her ear. "The water is still warm. Which means we don't have to go anywhere just yet."

"You're incredible, you know that?"

He pulled his hand from her and kissed her neck again. This time his teeth scraped across her sensitive skin, sending a delightful shiver through her. "It doesn't hurt that you're incredible, too."

They stayed in the tub together for a while, with Kirk holding her and whispering sweet words into her ear.

When she finally climbed out of the bathtub, he handed her a silky bathrobe and she put it on. She loved the luxurious feeling of the fabric on her hot skin.

Kirk wrapped a towel around his hips and smiled at her. "How are you feeling?"

"Wonderful." She slid her arms around him and looked deep into his eyes. "How had your day been since I went to my therapy session?"

His hands roamed down her body to her hips. "Nothing has changed since this morning, so I don't want you stressed out about things you can't control. I'm going to make sure you spend the rest of the day relaxing, okay?"

"Are you sure? Because I know this leak has probably been tough for you."

He pressed a soft, gentle kiss to her lips. "Spending time with you is the only thing I want to do for the rest of the day."

Getting him to focus on work-related drama right now was futile. Not that she minded his attentiveness at all. Spending the rest of the day with him was her idea of heaven.

THE NEXT AFTERNOON, Kirk drove home and rushed into the mansion. Work had been nothing but emergency meetings about the leak. Half the senior staff wanted to go ahead and choose a temporary bank president regardless of the leak, while the other half wanted to slow down and focus on stopping the leaks before moving ahead. Either way, he hadn't told anybody about his suspicions about the leak. Telling them he thought the leaker was working for a corrupt former police chief to make a profit off bank shares would cause the kind of panic that ruined companies. Getting proof on the leaker's identity was the only way to solve this, and until his cousin got back to him with news on that front Kirk had no choice but to keep his suspicions to himself.

He found Bethany in the living room, sketching in her sketchbook on the sofa while she absently watched TV.

She turned to look at him and smiled. "You're home! How was work?"

"Ian just sent me a message about my parents. He says they just left their bail hearing and the local news should have the details. Maybe this means our parents will be getting out of jail today." Kirk reached for the remote and changed the channel.

Apprehension flickered in her eyes. "I got a call from my brother earlier today, too. My father's new lawyer is trying to work with the judge, but I figured out something that's making me kind of nervous."

"What did you figure out?" he asked with a frown.

"The judge working on my father's bail appeal is the same judge who presided over my dad's case ten years ago." She bit her lip. "I don't think that judge has a good opinion about my father at all. What if he wants to make an example of him?"

If the judge was as harsh as she seemed to believe then his own parents might be in trouble, too. "We have to hope for the best. Your father has a better lawyer now. That will give him a better chance of making bail."

Kirk took a seat beside her, reaching for her hand. As stressful as a situation like this was, he was going to do everything in his power to comfort her through this. With his free hand he flipped through the channels until he stopped at a local news show.

A news anchor was reporting the day's events. A breaking news bulletin suddenly flashed on the screen.

"Two separate bail hearings were held today for banking tycoons Bruno and Vivian Sterling, and disgraced former Livingston Bank CEO Lloyd Livingston. While the judge ordered that both Sterlings be allowed out on bail, he did not granted bail to Lloyd Livingston. Judge Crowley's rationale to deny bail was based on Lloyd Livingston's prior convictions. Livingston was recently released after serving a ten-year prison sentence for embezzlement and fraud. The Sterlings are expected to be released from jail within the next twenty-four hours. No trial date has been set, but sources say that charges against all the accused will include obstruction of justice and failure to report a crime."

Bethany pulled her hand away and clutched her chest. "This isn't happening. This can't be happening."

"Bethany, we'll fight until we get your father home—"

"No. Don't you see? The only reason my dad is still in jail is because of what your parents did to him." She sucked in an audible breath, her entire body shaking. "I've been such a fool."

"You haven't," he insisted. "This isn't your fault. I'm not going to let you feel guilty about something you didn't have anything to do with."

Her eyes glistened with tears. "I was so ready to root for you. To believe in you. Did you know that I actually started to want you to take over my father's bank? I wanted the bank in your hands because I thought you deserved it. Now I see that you winning means my father loses."

"It doesn't have to mean that." As he took her by the shoulders, her body stiffened at his touch. He pulled his hand back quickly, suddenly filled with guilt. Was Bethany right? Did his good fortune mean that her father had to pay a price for it? If he won, did that mean that someone had to lose?

"Maybe it doesn't have to, but that's not how the world works." Her lower lip trembled. "This is why my mother thinks I'm a traitor. It's probably why she leaked my location to the press. I was upset at her for doing it, yet now I see why. My family hates me. They all hate me and I don't blame them."

"This isn't your fault," he said firmly.

"If it isn't my fault then whose fault is it?" she demanded in a shaky voice. "I actually wanted my father's enemy to succeed. What kind of daughter does that?"

Her pain and anger toward him stung. It twisted his insides until he could barely stand to breathe.

"You're a better daughter than any of our parents could ever deserve." Even though he should probably be angry at her outburst, he understood where it was coming from. For the entire time they had known each other, Bethany had been cornered. Forced to make an impossible choice between her relationship with him and a relationship with her parents. That kind of strain was unfair for anyone, and it was especially unfair to her.

Shoving his anger aside, he took a chance and reached for her hand again. This time she didn't stiffen or pull away. That was an encouraging sign. He hoped it meant that she was ready to keep listening. "This is the last thing I wanted for your father," he continued. "Though we're supposed to be enemies, I don't want your father to suffer. Not if my parents are able to walk free from something they must have had a hand in."

Tears rolled down her cheeks. "My father will never forgive me. What if he doesn't ever get out of jail? What if he's sent back to prison for the rest of his life?" A sob tore from her throat.

"We're going to fight to make sure that doesn't happen," he said firmly. "You can be angry with me if you want, but I'm sticking by you no matter how angry you get. If you want to get your father out of jail, then from now on that's my priority."

"You've helped enough," she said coldly. "If my father knew how much you've already done to help me, it would destroy him. His pride would never be able to survive the shame of it."

"You... you're ashamed of accepting my help?"

"I'm ashamed that my father has to depend on his enemies to get out of jail." Angrily, she swiped at her tears. "How would your parents feel if they had to rely on my father to get out of jail?"

The embarrassment of something like that would probably kill them. Though he was reluctant to admit that truth to her.

Before he could say something to soothe her obvious pain, his phone rang. He pulled it out of his pocket. His cousin. Which meant this was important. He'd have to take the call.

"Ian, I just found out the news," he said.

"My dad is ecstatic," Ian said. "I'm so freaking glad they're finally out. We've got to celebrate, Cousin."

"Celebrate?" Kirk's eyes narrowed. "Ian, Lloyd Livingston is still in jail. I can't celebrate."

"Oh. Shit." Ian sighed. "I forgot Bethany would take that part hard. So... you're not happy your parents are getting out?"

His eyes flicked over to Bethany. Fresh tears were spilling down her cheeks. "I don't know," he murmured. "I'm glad my parents are out. It's just that if Bethany isn't happy, then neither am I."

"I hear you." Ian sighed again. "Now I feel bad about having to tell you the rest of the news. It isn't great."

His heart slammed in his chest. "What is it?"

"I interviewed everyone who was at the meeting, and right now I don't think anybody leaked the news about the temporary president to the press."

"You're sure?" Kirk frowned.

"Unless these people are the best actors I've ever met then, yeah, I'm sure. I'm sorry, Kirk. I mean, maybe someone emailed something that accidentally got into the wrong hands," Ian said. "We could ask cyber security to take a look."

"Contacting the bank's cyber security department is the first thing I'm doing tomorrow," Kirk said. "Thanks for calling, Ian. I appreciate everything you've done for me lately. I owe you big time."

"Hey, you've always helped me when I was in a jam," Ian said. "This is what family is for. Call me the minute your parents get out."

"Will do." With that, Kirk hung up and turned his attention back to Bethany.

She'd stopped crying, though her face was still tear-streaked. "Oh, crap. I'm going to have to call my mother," she said. "That's if she'll even take my call."

"You should message her before you call," he suggested. "It might be safer to gauge her reaction that way."

"My poor brother. After everything he tried to do to get my dad out." Her shoulders heaved as her face twisted into a look of raw anguish. Tears glistened in her eyes again, but they didn't fall this time. "I really thought we had a chance to get my father home. If he never gets out, I don't know what I'll do."

"Did the charges make sense to you?" he asked gently. "Obstruction and failure to report a crime don't sound bad enough for your father to be locked away for the rest of his life."

"You heard what the news said about the judge. My dad has a prior conviction. There's no way the justice system is going to show him any mercy."

His heart plummeted. It was likely that the judge was trying to make an example of her father. Which meant the rest of the system probably felt the same way. "Maybe my parents will be able to get him out."

She shot him an incredulous look. "Kirk, I'm an optimist but even I don't believe that. We have to face the truth. Our parents hate each other. There's absolutely no way they'd help each other get out of prison. This feud between them is still destroying everything." With a sigh she buried her head in her hands. "Here I am worrying about my dad, when something has probably been going on at the bank." She lowered her hands as she turned to face him. "What was your cousin saying about cyber security? Is everything at the bank okay?"

"Don't worry about the bank. Right now, we should focus on your dad," he said.

"My dad is connected to the bank, remember? For all we know, whoever leaked to the press got my father sent to jail again."

"Cyber security..." He paused, the words sending a memory flashing through his mind. "Bethany, that's it. I think I know where the leak to the press came from."

Chapter 12

"You know who the leak is?" she asked with a gasp. Hope made her wipe the rest of her tears away and sit up straighter. There was a chance the person was connected to Damien Kemp. Which meant that, ultimately, they were connected to all the shady dealings at the bank. Another major clue in everything could help her save her father. "Who is it?"

"Even though I'm confident about my theory, this is just a hunch," he cautioned. "Right now, I don't have enough proof."

"At least it's a lead," she said. "Is it one of the board members who was in that meeting with you? Or... what about your dad? I doubt your father leaked since he's been in jail this whole time, but didn't he know the final candidates?"

"I don't think it was my father or someone that high up, though I haven't ruled those people out completely." His brow furrowed as a thoughtful expression settled on his handsome face. "I think I've been going about this all wrong. I've been looking at all the board members and senior staff members that I swore to secrecy. Ian doesn't seem to think they're guilty, and I trust his judgment. In fact, he's one of the few people I still trust at all."

She chewed her lip. "So if it isn't a board member or a bank shareholder, who could it possibly have been? The only other person left is me, and I swear I never told a soul."

"I believe you, Bethany," he said gently. "I know our relationship started off pretty rocky, but I trust you now. Don't ever doubt that, okay?"

Guilt and regret gnawed at her. She had been unfair to him earlier. It wasn't his fault that her father hadn't been granted bail. Kirk wasn't responsible for what his parents had done. Just like she wasn't responsible for the money that had been embezzled ten years ago.

If she could spend all these years resenting the media for accusing her of being in on her father's crimes, it was totally hypocritical for her to pin the blame on Kirk now. Her fear and hurt over her father getting arrested again had pushed her over the edge. She didn't know how she could possibly make amends for lashing out at him the way she had.

"I don't doubt it," she finally said. "Which is why I'm so sorry for letting my temper and emotions get the best of me. I shouldn't have lost my temper with you. Especially after you paid for my father's lawyer. Instead of thanking you and being grateful for all your help, I lashed out at you. That was wrong and I'm so sorry, Kirk."

He reached over to caress her cheek, sending sparks prickling across her skin. Even with all the turmoil of her emotions, one tender touch from him heightened her senses.

"You don't have to apologize," he said. "You're going through a lot right now with your dad and the rest of your family."

"I had no right to take it out on you, though."

His hand slid down to cup her chin. "I accept your apology. Now... don't you want to hear my theory?"

"Of course I do." She gave him a shaky smile.

He pulled his hand away to reach for his phone. "Give me a second." Without explanation, he stood up and exited the living room for a long moment.

When he came back to sit down beside her again, she stared at him, bewildered. "What's going on?"

"I have a theory and I can't take any chances that someone might be listening in," he said. "So, I left my cell phone in my study just in case."

Her eyes widened. "You think your phone was bugged?" she asked in a low voice, suddenly paranoid.

Kirk nodded. "That's the best way to put it. Yes, I think someone tampered with it."

"How? Your phone is always with you, so who could have gotten their hands on it?"

"A few days ago a security officer from the bank's cyber security department came to make sure my devices were secure. At the time I didn't think anything of it. My parents had just been arrested and nobody knew why. It was best to make sure that there hadn't been some kind of breach, or worse." He leaned back and frowned. "Now I'm starting to wonder if that was a mistake."

She chewed her bottom lip. "So, you think there's a chance that someone in the bank's cyber security department managed to get access to your devices to get sensitive information about the bank? But why? What would a security officer have to gain from all that? I doubt some computer geek is spending their time making shady deals with bank stocks."

"If he works for Damien Kemp, he has a lot of gain. If Kemp managed to become the city's chief of police, getting a cyber security guy to do his dirty work wouldn't be that hard," he reminded her. "Kemp has had enough leverage to come after our parents in the past. And they're some of the most powerful people in the city. Using a cyber security officer like Edward Pryce wouldn't be a challenge for him at all."

"That makes sense. Plus, Kemp was able to rise up the ranks of the police force and go against San Diego's mayor. It would be easy for him to bribe someone in cyber security," she mused.

"Or blackmail him. Think about it. With his expertise, there's a chance that the cyber security officer has hacked into one or two places he shouldn't have and—"

"And Kemp being the former police chief means he'd have easy access to criminal records," she finished for him. "But Kirk, we stood up to him at the auction. We took all that money away from Damien so that the criminals he works for would come after him for losing it. Why go through all the trouble of accessing your devices, when he has to worry about his own safety?"

"My guess is Damien is trying to save himself," Kirk answered. "If he can get the money back in some way, he might take the risk. From the way he talked about his bosses, they're the kind of people who get violent with anyone who crosses them. If Damien was scared of retaliation for his failure, he might have come up with a brilliant plan to pay them back and possibly save his life."

Suddenly, his theory started to make even more sense to her. Though she didn't know Kemp that well, from her limited time with him she sensed that he was cunning. Patient, but relentless. He'd do anything to survive. Anything. "So, you think Damien found a way to make company stocks plummet long enough for his bosses to buy them cheaply."

"Right. That way they'd either have enough shares in the bank to own a significant chunk of it, or they'd sell them off at an incredibly high profit." He sighed heavily. "Either way, a huge part of the bank could end up being owned by someone I don't even know."

Ice-cold fear crept down her spine. Somehow this was worse than the Sterlings taking her father's bank away. At least she had known the Sterlings. Plus, Kirk's parents had worked at the bank for years before they took it over. Whoever got a hold of all those bank shares was likely to be way more dangerous than Kirk's parents.

"So, what are you going to do now?" she asked, fighting to keep her voice calm. As nerve-wracking as this was, this wasn't the time to panic. "Are you going to get rid of your devices? Or have a cyber security expert look at them?"

"Well, my laptop is the most important device that the cyber security officer had access to," he said. "Thank goodness he didn't find a way into the desktop in my study. That's the most important device I own. However, I'm going to have to find a way to increase the security on the desktop by tomorrow afternoon. But dealing with my laptop is trickier, especially since we can't trust the police to handle this properly."

"Laptop..." A distant roar sounded in her ears. The healed gash on her forehead started to throb, the painful ghost of a memory invading her mind. Hands from the past reached for her and she shrank back in terror.

Her heart started to race so fast she thought it might explode and break her ribs. Chest tightening painfully with panic, she grabbed hold of the arm of the sofa to keep herself steady.

"Bethany?" He gripped her shoulder, voice filled with concern. "What's wrong? Is it your head again?"

She sucked down a breath, shaking her head. "No. I mean, yes." Squeezing her eyes shut for a moment, she forced down another breath. "The attack. Kirk, I remember what happened."

⸺⚫⸺

FOR DAYS THE ATTACK had been a black hole in her memory. A terrifying gap in time she had desperately wanted to remember. Now, part of her wished she hadn't remembered at all.

"What happened?" Even though he was sitting right beside her, Kirk sounded like he was a million miles away.

The shock of regaining her memories had probably dulled her senses. Everything around her either seemed to move in slow motion or sounded distant to her ears.

"I was walking back to my apartment after a trip to the convenience store. That's when he attacked me." As the memories came flooding back, she felt like she was watching the whole scene unfold on a screen in front of her.

She had unlocked her apartment door, walked inside, and had then been grabbed from behind. In terror she had struggled against the strongest, coldest hands she had ever felt in her life. Somehow she had wrenched free of him. All the while, her attacker had shouted at her. Threatened to kill her if she didn't hand over her belongings.

At first she had thought he had been there to take her valuables, but finally she had spun around and seen him. Recognized him.

"It was Damien Kemp," she said.

A fire burned in the distance. It took her a second to realize that it was the hatred burning in Kirk's green eyes. "So the bastard didn't send one of his thugs to do his dirty work like he usually does. He attacked you personally."

She nodded. "Yes. He kept asking me 'Where is it?' Over and over. He was all red-faced and sweaty. Like he was scared out of his mind. More scared than I was."

"What did he want?"

"He wanted to get the money back," she replied. "The money we recovered from him at the auction."

"And he thought you had millions of dollars stashed in your apartment?" Kirk asked in surprise.

"No. He wanted to get his hands on my laptop. Damien thought that he could get the money back if he had my laptop to access my bank account," she said. "He must have been really desperate."

Images of Damien lunging at her flashed in her head. He had demanded she hand over her laptop. In defiance, she had refused. Refused to give anything to someone so vile and corrupt. That money hadn't been his to take. Thousands of people's lives had been destroyed, and she had refused to let Damien Kemp add to their suffering.

"You didn't hand over your laptop, did you?" Kirk asked.

She lifted her chin. "I didn't. He had no right to demand anything after all the lives he ruined."

"But Bethany, we took the money from Kemp using *my* laptop. You could have just given him the laptop to get him to leave."

"If I hadn't put up a fight, he would have figured out that the laptop was useless," she breathed. "He would have come after you. I couldn't let that happen to you, Kirk. I couldn't let him hurt you."

He took her hands in his and brought them to his lips. The warmth of his kiss across her knuckles chased away some of the chill of her fear. "Kemp could have killed you for that," he said in a tone she had never heard him use before. That was a frantic, strangled anguish in his voice, and beneath it a barely-contained rage.

"He-he tried to." Her throat tightened with emotion. The trauma of that day mixed with a palatable relief that she had survived the attack.

After she had flat out refused to give him the laptop, Damien had chased her into the kitchen. There had been a scuffle. Then, in his frustrated rage, Damien had grabbed her face with his huge hands and smashed her forehead repeatedly against the side of a granite countertop.

"The gash in my forehead... Damien bashed my head into one of the countertops in the kitchen." A tremor made her pause long enough to gain her bearings. "My entire body just went numb after that. I crashed to the floor. Then he ran out of the kitchen."

From her place on the cold kitchen floor, she had heard Damien Kemp ransacking her apartment. Ripping the place apart in his desperation to get his hands on her laptop. The shock of the blow to her head had all but paralyzed her for what felt like hours.

Finally, Damien had walked back into the kitchen and held up her laptop triumphantly.

"When he came back into the kitchen after finding my laptop he said that, even though he wished he could make you and me pay for stealing from him, his accomplice would take care of the rest," she said with a shudder.

"His accomplice?"

She nodded. "Yes. He told me that there was no point in watching our backs because we'd never see his accomplice coming. Then he laughed and took off."

"So the bastard left you on the floor like that to suffer." Releasing her from his grasp he stood up, his lip curled with contempt. "Kemp is going to pay for this."

"You saved me," she reminded him gently. There was no telling what he might do in his anger, and she'd do anything to stop him before he did something dangerous. She refused to let Kirk put himself in harm's way on her behalf. With her father still in jail, she couldn't bear to lose anyone else. "I passed out right after Damien left, but you found me just in time. That's all that matters now."

"Your safety is what matters," he growled. "As long as Kemp and his goons are out there, you aren't safe."

"Kirk, promise me you won't do anything reckless," she pleaded. "If you can find it in your heart to be civil to my family, then at least take the time to come up with a plan. Don't go into this with guns blazing."

"Damien hasn't given us much choice." He rolled up the sleeves of his jacket. "You've just said that Kemp has an accomplice. That proves my theory that he's been getting help from inside the bank. His accomplice is obviously the cyber security officer I told you about."

"We've only just gotten news that your parents are getting out of jail," she said. "Focus on that. Trust me when I say this: The time you have with them is so precious." While she couldn't deny the resentment that settled over her, she truly wanted Kirk to reconnect with this parents. His relationship with them had been strained because of her, yet now they were getting another chance.

Blowing out a frustrated breath, he stopped in his tracks to fix his gaze on her. "My parents will never forgive me if I let the bank slip through my fingers. Losing the bank will destroy them. Damien is obviously trying to steal his money back. He might even be planning to buy enough shares to take the bank away from my family. We don't have the luxury of time. Waiting isn't an option right now."

"What are you even planning? How are going to stop the leak from doing more damage?" she asked, dreading the answer already.

He kept his hard gaze on her, the serious expression on his face sending an anxious shiver down her spine. The look in his eye was a sign that his mind was already made up. She couldn't talk him down. Couldn't stop him. All she could do was slow him down. For now.

"I'm going to confront the cyber security officer," he said. "And I can't trust the entire cyber security department. Not after one of their own has abused my trust like this. I don't have any other choice but to fire every single person in that department. Even if it kills me to have to go through with it."

If he was contemplating something that extreme, then she knew just how worried he was about losing control of the bank completely. "Won't something like that make the other employees angry?"

"It might," he said with a heavy sigh. "I don't take any pleasure in doing this, Bethany. But I have to save the bank from possible destruction. Whoever Kemp works for might take it over to siphon money out of it and leave it in ruins. If that happens, it won't just be the employees in the cyber security department who are out of a job. Thousands of bank employees would have to be laid off and our clients would suffer."

"At least get more evidence," she begged. His reasons for wanting to come out swinging made sense. But it was clear that he would only get one chance at stopping Damien Kemp and his accomplice. If for some reason he wound up accusing the wrong person, Damien Kemp's actual accomplice might realize they were in danger of being caught and skip town, too. "If you get more evidence, you'll know who Kemp's accomplice is for sure. There won't be any doubts getting in your way."

"There are always doubts." His eyes shifted from hers. She followed his gaze as it landed on a huge photograph above the mantel of the stone fireplace.

It was an enormous photo of his parents. One of those photos that was so detailed that it had to have been taken by an elite magazine photographer. His father was seated in an antique chair, cigar in hand, while his wife, Vivian Sterling, stood behind him with her hands on her husband's shoulders. Even in photographs Bruno and Vivian Sterling exuded power.

Not the kind of power her own family had merely inherited. The kind of power that they had ruthlessly seized with their own hands. Just looking at their hard stares and the ever-so-faint, knowing smiles intimidated her.

"You don't want to disappoint them," she said softly. For him, this was about protecting not only her but all the other people he cared about as well. His parents.

Taking a deep breath, she threw back her shoulders and stood up. There was only one way to get what they both wanted. Only one way to save the bank *and* be as cautious about it as possible. She was just stunned that it had come to this. Because, right now, she was about to tell him to do something she never thought she'd ever suggest.

As she walked over to his side, she felt her own apprehension cling to her the way it had ever since her attack. She reached for his hand, catching his attention long enough for their eyes to meet.

"I can't believe I'm about to say this, but..." She bit her lip. What she was about to say could lead to her losing her family once and for all. "The only way to do this right is to ask your parents for help."

Chapter 13

He jerked back in surprise. "Are you serious?"

"I wouldn't joke about something like this, Kirk." She tilted her head, studying him for one silent moment. "Suggesting that we go to *your parents* for help should show you that I'm being completely serious."

"We?" His eyes narrowed on her. He didn't like the sound of this. Not one bit.

Her eyes glinted with a determination that pushed his concern for her safety to the edge of panic. "We're in this together," she said, like it was the most obvious thing in the world.

"Your doctor gave you specific orders to avoid stress." He shoved his hands into his pockets and scowled down at her. If she insisted on being stubborn, he was going to have to use every weapon he had to talk her out of it. "I'm handling this on my own."

"No. You're not." She crossed her arms and returned his glare with one of her own.

Reminding her of her doctor's orders wasn't having the effect he'd hoped for. Time to try a different tactic. "You have enough on your plate with your dad. Now that he's been denied bail again, your next step should be to focus on getting the charges against him dropped."

"Oh, don't worry. I'll definitely focus on my father. Nothing is going to stop me from putting my family back together, no matter how long it takes," she said. "But I'm also not going to let my father's bank fall into the wrong hands. Your parents taking the bank from him is one thing. Letting my father's hard work and sacrifices go to a band of shady criminals is another. At least your parents earned the bank without beating people unconscious to do it."

"So, not only are you willing to defy your doctor's orders, but you're willing to work with my parents as well?" He shook his head in disbelief. "Bethany, even though you've forgiven my parents, I know there's a part of you that resents them now that they've made bail."

"It's the only way to get you to slow down and do this the right way," she said. "I know when you're about to do something reckless. Your parents are cunning enough to come up with a plan that will keep you out of trouble."

"You mean a plan that's much slower and much more cautious." He rubbed his eyes with his palms in annoyance. "I can't believe you're actually suggesting this."

"We have to team up with your parents to make sure we stop Kemp's accomplice," she said. "Your parents know things about the bank that neither of us do."

"Are you sure you're up for this?" he asked. "I mean, you do realize that they won't help get your father out of jail, right?"

Her chin quivered for a second before she wrestled for control, turning her face as unreadable as possible. "I realize that."

Asking his parents for help meant that Bethany was desperate to protect him from his own impulses. The thought of slowing things down didn't sit well with him, but neither did screwing up their one shot to get this right. Bethany had made a good point. Accusing the cyber security officer of leaking confidential information with such flimsy evidence could easily backfire. If Pryce really was the accomplice, he could shrug off the accusation. Worse, if Edward Pryce wasn't the accomplice, the real culprit could quickly cover their tracks and avoid getting caught.

She stared at him expectantly.

His heart squeezed so tightly that it hurt to breathe. The last time he had let her in on his plans to protect the bank, Damien Kemp had attacked her. Attacked her so badly that she was still recovering. Failing her again was unthinkable.

"What's wrong, Kirk?" she asked gently. "What aren't you telling me?"

"Finding you in your kitchen was the worst moment of my whole life." He cleared his throat, trying to get rid of the lump that was forming. "And it could have been so much worse."

"You know, I worry about your safety, too," she said. "Yet, through everything we've been through together, I've trusted your strength. All I ask is that you trust mine."

He moved closer to her and took her small, delicate hand. "If we come up with a plan to take down Kemp's accomplice, we also have to find out if his bosses really are trying to take over the bank."

"We?" A tiny smile played on her lush lips.

"Yes. We." He gave her hand a gentle squeeze. "Plus, we have to find a way to get your dad out of jail."

"Your parents won't like that." Sadness flickered in her blue eyes and her smile vanished. "If we help my dad, your parents might not agree to help us come up with a plan."

"Then we won't tell them." He turned his attention back to the portrait above the fireplace mantel. His parents stared back at him with their unseeing eyes.

His interpretation of the portrait had often depended on his mood. Sometimes the glint in their eyes inspired him to keep fighting. Other times he would swell with pride at seeing two people who had come from nothing persevere against all odds. Right now their gazes looked stern, as if they were silently judging him for all his choices.

The bank could easily slip away. Their fortune gone with it. All because he had decided to stand up to the shady characters his parents had put up with for years.

"So, when do we go talk to them?" she asked.

He arched a quizzical eyebrow. "We? *We* aren't saying anything to my parents. *I* am."

Her jaw dropped. "You're going to ask for their help alone? But we just agreed—"

"I agreed that we can work to save the bank together," he finished for her. "I didn't agree to you dealing with my parents directly."

"I get it. You're still not ready to tell them about us."

"That's not it at all." His jaw tightened as realization struck him. Even though he wasn't going to tell his parents about helping Lloyd Livingston, there was one truth he was going to have to reveal. Even if it meant ruining the bank in the process.

"I'm going to tell them," he continued. "I'm going to stop hiding. Stop keeping the truth from them. It's time to tell my parents the truth about us."

———◉———

"YOU'RE REALLY GOING through with it," she said in surprise.

"Damn right I am." He guided her hand to his chest to show her how serious he was. His heart was beating so fast, he was almost certain she could feel it hammering beneath her fingertips.

"But you're the one who broke things off when your mother found out about us the first time," she reminded him. "Are you really ready to tell your parents that we're back together?"

"I'm ready."

"Telling them in the middle of all this chaos might just make things worse," she warned. "What if they don't agree to help you after you tell them we're dating?"

"I have to tell them about us because we might not get a chance like this ever again," he said.

She shook her head in confusion.

"Even though I hate to admit it, my parents are in a much weaker position now that they've been arrested. If I tell them now, it'll be much tougher for either of them to justify coming after you," he said.

"Wow." Her eyes widened as their gazes met. Held. Recognition danced in her eyes, as if she was seeing him for the first time in ages. "Sometimes I forget how ruthless you are."

Releasing his hold on her hand to grip her waist, Kirk pulled her close. So close that the heat of her body sent his pulse racing before he could form a coherent thought. "When it comes to protecting you, Bethany, only I know how ruthless I can be."

As she reached for his lapels, she trembled in his arms. That tell-tale sign of her desire. The same desire that was welling up in him now.

With a stifled groan, he conquered her hot mouth with his. The kiss was fiery. With a raging heat that contrasted incredibly with the sensation of her soft lips crushed against his. He had been so focused on protecting her that he'd neglected the one thing he could never get tired of: Exploring her body.

No matter how many times he tasted her ripe, sweet mouth, he always learned something new about her. Learned more about what made her shiver and gasp for more. Suddenly she nipped at his lower lip, her teeth grazing him slightly. The sweet, sharp ache spurred him on and he forced her lips apart with his tongue.

She leaned into him, so close that he felt her hardened nipples against his chest.

Desire shot to his groin and his hands were all over her. Running up her soft body as he let his hands brush against her breasts, then move down as he cupped her ass. Then back up again as he slipped his hands up her shirt to touch her silky-smooth skin.

A little gasp escaped her and she pulled back, tearing her delectable mouth away.

He winced. "You're not ready. I'm sorry. We can slow down. Or stop, if that's what you want."

"No," she said with a shake of her head. "I want you. Right now. Here." Her voice was a husky, inviting purr.

"Here?" He stared at her in shock, taking in the stark need that was plain her face. Eyes burning bright with longing. Cheeks flushed with desire. Lips curving into a seductive smile. "One of the maids could catch us."

"Kirk, if I don't have you within the next thirty seconds I'm going to explode."

Thirty seconds left no room for racing upstairs to his bedroom or rushing out back to the guesthouse. And right here in the living room was out of the question. That left only one option.

"Come with me," he ordered. With his hand on the small of her back, he rushed her out of the living room and into his home study.

The fire in her blue eyes blazed hotter as she realized what they were about to do. "Where do you want me?" she asked, giving him a teasing smile.

He shut the door. "On my desk."

She let out a breathless high-pitched laugh, halfway between a giggle and a sigh. Then, she slowly walked over to his desk and leaned against it. Running her pink tongue across her lips, she let out another breathless laugh.

Damn, she was the sexiest woman he had ever known. And he'd never been so hard in his life.

Walking over to her against the strain of his erection was a minor miracle. When he stopped in front of her, she smiled. Holding his gaze, she wantonly reached her hands up her skirt and tugged her panties down.

As the bit of lacy fabric slid down her long legs, he almost passed out from the provocative sight. She was so impossibly seductive, and he couldn't believe she was all his.

The blush in her cheeks deepened as she climbed up to sit on his desk, propping herself up with her hands. Slowly, agonizingly slowly, she spread her legs. "I'm ready," she breathed.

His pulse started to race. The blood in his veins smoldered with desire. He had to get out of his pants quickly before he lost the ability to think. With a few deft motions he unbuckled his belt, unbuttoned his pants, and lowered his boxer briefs enough to grab hold of his erection.

She swallowed hard, and he saw the way her pulse quickened against her throat. Within seconds, he closed the gap between them until he gripped his desk with one hand, his throbbing manhood in the other.

Her eyes met his and she hooked her leg around his hips, pulling him closer to her. "Take me." Her plea was practically a whimper.

Kirk didn't need her to beg him again. One hard thrust was all it took for him to be impossibly deep inside her. The slick, wet heat that enveloped him felt so damn good that, for one second, he thought he might pass out from the pleasure of it.

Moaning loudly she tossed her head back, her long locks of blond hair swirling around her face like a halo of solid gold. The ecstasy etched on her face nearly made him come right then and there.

But he couldn't. Not after she had been so eager to have him. Right now, he was going to have to fight for control while he pleasured her as thoroughly as she deserved. Desperate to control his pace, he rocked into her with slow, hard strokes.

She met each stroke as she rolled her hips, her breath coming out in loud, needy gasps. "Oh, hell. *Yes.*"

Having her like this filled him with a primal need. An ache to make his body a part of hers. To make her body a part of his. The pleasure slamming through him wasn't just his. It was hers. He felt her own pleasure as she clenched around him, pulling him to the brink of heart-stopping release.

A ragged cry tore from her throat, her body quivering as he sped up his punishing pace. She climaxed, moaning his name. Ecstasy gripped him so hard that he climaxed right after her.

As he fought to catch his breath, he reached down to brush her hair out of her face. She smiled up at him and tugged at his tie to pull him down for a kiss. He groaned at the softness of her lips, and as he started to drown in the taste of her he knew that he never wanted this moment to end.

Chapter 14

"**I**'m picking my parents up today," he told her over breakfast the following morning.

She had been messaging Jane, approving furnishing ideas for the shop now that several months' rent had been paid for. Setting her phone down on the dining table, she turned her attention to him. "You mean... pick them up from jail?"

He nodded grimly. "Picking up my own parents from jail sounds pretty terrible when you think about it, but yeah. Their lawyer called me earlier this morning and we agreed that I should be the one to do it. Then I can drive them home. If I let a chauffeur drive them and the media gets a photo, that's not going to look good for either of them."

"I hadn't even thought of that." She grimaced. A wealthy couple getting whisked away from jail by their chauffeur would not go down well. Outrage would be off the charts.

The sound of the doorbell ringing made her pause. "Are you expecting someone this morning?"

"Yes. That's probably Ian," Kirk explained. "He'll be coming with me as a show of support. We figured it would be good press."

"So, you'll be telling your parents about us later today?" She reached for a teaspoon to spoon some sugar into her cup of tea, hoping to distract herself from her nerves. They'd agreed to tell his parents, but that didn't stop the butterflies in her stomach. The last time Kirk's mother had found out about their relationship, she had gotten Bethany arrested on flimsy charges.

If there was a repeat of that, there was no telling what lengths his parents would go to this time. The hatred between their two families seemed to get worse over time, not better. She'd have a better chance of putting things right if she knew everything that had happened ten years ago.

Even now, despite unraveling some of the shadiness that had gone on at the bank, she still wasn't completely sure about her father's role in the drama of their lives. Had he really embezzled all that money? Or had the Sterlings framed him so that they could keep control of the bank for themselves?

"I will." He took her free hand and brought her palm to his lips. The brush of his mouth against her skin sent a flash of heat rippling through her body. When he released her hand he fixed an attentive gaze on her, his green eyes filled with worry. "Besides all that, how are you feeling now that your memory has come back?"

"Anxious," she admitted. "Though I also feel relieved."

"Really?"

She nodded. "Yes. Now that I can remember what happened, things don't feel as uncertain. The stress of not remembering is gone. I can also schedule another session with the therapist now that it's come back to me." "Good. You doctor did advise you to talk to a professional, so that's a good idea," he said. "But I'm always here if you ever need to talk about anything, okay?"

"Okay," she murmured.

His concern for her melted her heart. During the years after her father had gone to prison, she had almost given up on having someone genuinely in her corner. Genuinely on her side for a change. Somehow she had found that with the most unlikely man imaginable.

Though her relationship with her already-broken family was more strained because of her relationship with Kirk, she wouldn't change it for the world. The way Kirk cherished her had completely changed her life. Given her hope that she had nearly lost. His care and concern for her was more precious than anything.

Resentment had plagued her dreams last night because, even though Kirk's parents were getting out of jail, her father wasn't. Kirk's compassion for her despite the feud was helping her deal with her negative emotions this morning.

Ian appeared in the dining room and greeted them. "How are you doing, Bethany? Feeling better, I hope?"

"I do feel better," she said. "I'm getting stronger each day." There was no point in telling Ian about going back to the hospital, or her regained memory. Those details were way too private to share with him, no matter how fond she was of him now.

"Glad to hear it." Ian grabbed a seat beside her and reached for some grapes. "I heard about your dad not making bail, Bethany. If you want my advice, the best way to get him out now is to fight to have the charges dropped completely."

"You...you want to help me get my dad out?" she asked in shock. Even though he didn't stand to inherit her father's old bank, Ian was still a Sterling. That one fact created an uneasy tension between them even if they both did their best to ignore it.

Ian paused to chew on a grape. "It'll make you happy, right?"

Her eyebrows went up, the shock mounting. Ian's deep concern for her father and her feelings was unexpected. "Yes. Right."

"So, if you're happy, then Kirk is happy," Ian explained. "That's what really matters."

"But Kirk's parents will be furious if my father gets out of jail," she pointed out gently.

"Speaking of which, Kirk, shouldn't we be heading out to pick them up?" Ian asked, looking at his watch.

"Yes, we should." Kirk shot his cousin a warning glance. "Whatever you do, don't mention Bethany or her father to my parents. Let me do most of the talking today."

"Sure, you've got it," Ian said, rising to his feet. "You coming?"

"Give me a second. I want to say goodbye to Bethany."

"No problem. I'll go warm up the car," Ian said with a nod before heading out of the dining room.

"It's nice to have his support," she said. "I do hope everything goes smoothly for your family today."

He stood up to grab his jacket from the back of his chair. "What are your plans for today anyway?"

The question caught her off guard. Something about the way he asked sounded more like an interrogation than an innocuous question. "Oh. Well, I'll have to call my old alma mater to ask them to move my fashion show and mentorship with the students to a later date. Being in the hospital has thrown my schedule off." She sighed heavily.

"I know you had committed to the fashion show, but getting rest is the best thing you can do," he said as he shrugged into his jacket. "Are you planning on doing anything else?"

Frustrated, she pushed her plate way and looked up at him. "Kirk, why don't you just ask me what you want to ask me?"

"I'm just making sure you don't do anything strenuous while you're still recovering," he explained.

"Strenuous? Oh, you mean like what we did yesterday on your desk?" she teased.

"*Bethany.*" His tone was a warning, but she could swear she saw his lips twitch.

She laughed. "Today, I'll just make some phone calls and send text messages." Her smile faded as she remembered what she had planned on doing later today. "I'll send my mom and my brother a message. Hopefully my brother will update me on my dad and what his lawyer's strategy is now. I won't risk a phone call, because I'm not sure how they'll react to me since my dad hasn't made bail." A call from her could just remind them that she was dating Kirk. That would only fan the flames of their hatred for the Sterling family.

"So that's it?" he asked. "You're not thinking of going down to the shop to help with the furnishing or something crazy like that?"

"Not today," she promised. "Though I'll be throwing myself back into work the minute my doctor gives me the all-clear."

"Good." He leaned down to give her a gentle kiss on the forehead. "As long as you're listening to your doctor's orders."

She smiled in spite of his obsession with protecting her. Having him so concerned for her would always touch her heart, no matter how infuriating it was sometimes. "Good luck with everything today."

"Thanks." He kissed her forehead again. "Enjoy your day."

Kirk gave her hand a final squeeze and then headed out of the dining room, leaving her alone. Her stomach knotted with worry. During breakfast she hadn't shown him how bad her anxiety was. There was no going back after Kirk told his parents about their relationship. With so many unknowns, there was no telling how badly Kirk's parents would react to the truth.

HE PULLED THE CAR TO a stop outside the city jail. Thankfully there didn't seem to be any sign of the press, just like his parents' lawyer had promised. No doubt their lawyer had convinced the media to stay away in exchange for some exclusive interviews with his parents. Either way, at least their release today wouldn't be a total circus.

"They're heading out," Ian said from the back seat.

Sure enough, his parents were stepping out of the rundown facility, their lawyer walking with them.

Seeing them for the first time in so many days made his chest tighten. Though they had been in jail for several days, it felt like he hadn't seen them in weeks. Then he remembered that, in his mother's case, he hadn't seen her since he had reunited with Bethany. His mother had been attending financial conferences all over the world before she was arrested.

Kirk opened the door and stepped out to greet his parents. Ian followed after and hugged them.

His father clapped him on the back and gave him a grateful smile. "Ian, Kirk, thanks for picking us up. I owe you two a lot for all the work you did to get us out."

"No problem, Dad."

"Oh, you decided to go with the white Bentley," his mother said as she leaned in to kiss his cheek. "Very sober choice."

"Your lawyer and I decided on it," he told her.

"Maybe you should have been a lawyer in another life." His mother looked him up and down, like she was trying to spot something. "Kirk, you look like death." Her brow creased with exaggerated concern. "Oh, darling, you shouldn't have worried so much about your father and me. We can take care of ourselves."

Of course he must have looked stressed. Because between fighting to get his parents out of jail and taking care of Bethany after that bastard Kemp had attacked her, it was a miracle he still had any energy left. Those problems didn't even include the mess going on with the leak in the Sterling Investment Bank.

"Your mother is right. Don't worry about us, Kirk," his father said. "We've been through worse."

"Exactly. My jail cell was more luxurious than the ratty apartments we lived in when you were growing up." His mother laughed. A little too loudly to his mind, but maybe she needed to make jokes go get through the stress of her arrest.

"Let's get you guys home." He opened a passenger door for his mother and helped her inside the car.

After he dropped his cousin off at work, he drove to his parents' mansion. He parked in front of the house, and they all got out to walk up to the front door. Before he lifted his hand to ring the bell, a maid opened the door to let them in to the mansion. As he crossed the marble floor of the foyer, he was reminded of just how immense the mansion was. His parents' home was even bigger than his place, and his mansion was huge.

Unlike his understated, elegantly decorated mansion, his parents' mansion was much gaudier with gold- plated furniture, huge crystal chandeliers, and bright, clashing colors.

Bathsheba, his mother's Pomeranian, came bounding up to them, barking like crazy.

"My poor baby, I've missed you so!" His mother, the most formidable woman he had ever known, dropped to her knees to make cooing noises at the dog. "I think I missed you most of all, my lovely, but don't tell anyone that." She scooped the dog up into her arms and carried it with her into the Moroccan-style living room.

His father sighed heavily. "I honestly think the only thing she worried about while she was in jail was that annoying animal."

"Doesn't surprise me," Kirk muttered.

They followed his mother into the living room. Already, she was instructing a maid to prepare the master bedroom.

As the maid exited Kirk sat down on a purple sofa, his father leaning over the coffee table to open his box of cigars. With a contented sigh his father grabbed a cigar, lit it with the lighter on the table, and took a puff. "It's good to be home," his father said as he took a seat beside his wife.

"That lawyer was money well-spent," his mom agreed.

"Too bad Livingston couldn't afford a good lawyer." His father chuckled and brought the cigar to his lips with a meaty hand. "He's still stuck in jail, the poor bastard."

Kirk fought to keep his face expressionless. His parents couldn't know that he had paid for Lloyd Livingston's new lawyer. Not if he wanted them to accept his news about Bethany. He cleared his throat. "Mom, Dad—we need to talk."

"That sounds ominous," his father said with a raised eyebrow.

His mother started to stroke the dog on her lap. "Is this about the bank?"

"Yes. But there's something I need to tell you before we talk business," Kirk replied.

His parents exchanged worried glances.

"Spit it out, son. Don't keep us in suspense," his dad prompted.

"It's about the woman I've been seeing." He leaned back in his seat, hoping to project a calm he suddenly didn't feel.

"You've been seeing someone?" His dad's eyes lit up. "That's wonderful. You're finally taking my advice. What kind of girl is she? Is she an heiress? A senator's daughter maybe? I bet she's the kind of girl who could open doors for us with all the old families in town."

Kirk raised his hands. "Don't get ahead of yourself, Dad. She's a fashion designer."

"Even better," his mom said. "I like a woman who works to earn her money. Sounds like a woman after my own heart. Better than that Livingston girl you were chasing around all those weeks ago."

If he didn't rip the band-aid off now, they were liable to go on with their fanciful visions. He took a deep breath and stared right at his mother. "It is the Livingston girl, as you so politely put it."

"What? You can't be serious! I thought I made myself perfectly clear!" his mother screeched. "Have you lost your mind again?"

"Livingston... as in *Lloyd* Livingston's daughter?" The cigar nearly dropped from his father's lips. "If this is some scheme of yours to ruin Lloyd—"

"It's not a scheme," Kirk said firmly. "Bethany *Walker* and I are together. She's my girlfriend, and nothing is going to come between us ever again."

"You didn't learn your lesson the first time around, did you?" His mom's face reddened. "Well, I'll be teaching you that lesson again. I'll have that little tramp back in jail in no time."

"You won't do a damn thing," Kirk said coldly.

Vivian's eyes widened in shock. "I cannot bear to hear your disrespect for one more second. How dare you speak to me that way in my own house!"

"You were the one who sent police officers to my house to arrest her weeks ago. That sure as hell doesn't sound respectful to me, Mom." Kirk's jaw clenched, his irritation mounting. "Can't you see how much damage your decisions caused?"

His mother swallowed hard. "I had to send the police after her. What if she was planning to steal from you? What if the little minx is a crook just like her father?"

"Are you kidding me?" Kirk demanded. "You two were just released from jail, yet you have the damn nerve to accuse other people of being criminals? Do you hear yourself?"

Indignation flashed in his mother's eyes. "I... how dare you!" she huffed.

"You're not going to call the cops on Bethany, because right now you have troubles of your own to sort out," Kirk said through gritted teeth. "You'll focus on your own problems instead of coming after my girlfriend."

"But what can she do for you?" his father asked. "She isn't an heiress anymore. Her parents might be from old families, but her father is rotting in jail and I've heard that her mother is a drunk. As far as I can tell, she has nothing useful to offer you."

"I'm not with her because of what I can get out of her," Kirk thundered. "I care about her. I know that's hard for you two to believe, considering how far gone you are now."

"What's that supposed to mean?" his mother sputtered.

"It means that, the more I look at you, the less I recognize you," Kirk bit out.

"You can't speak to us like that," his mother snapped, eyes blazing with anger. "Do you have any idea what we've sacrificed in order for you to have the life you have now? Your father and I spent years doing thankless work for those arrogant, self-important people. They treated us worse than they did their servants. Now, you have the nerve to parade their daughter around? Have you no shame? No sense of loyalty to this family?"

"Bethany isn't like her parents," he said forcefully. "If you knew her like I did, you'd see that immediately."

"I don't want to know her." His mother glared at him, nostrils flaring in rage. "I've had a very trying few days so you need to leave, Kirk. I don't want to discuss that woman right now—"

"Vivian, enough," his father said, cutting her off. "Let's at least hear him out."

His mother gasped. "You're taking his side? After everything the Livingstons put us through?"

"We've been acting high and mighty for too long." His father caught her hand and glanced at her. "You can't accuse the Livingston girl of being like her father. Not after all the things we've done."

"No. Bruno, no," his mother pleaded in a small voice. "Don't say anything else. You'll ruin everything."

"Take a look around," his dad said sternly. "We barely made bail, the bank is on shaky ground, and worst of all our own son has been hiding his girlfriend from us. Look at us. Our family needs to be united right now, and instead we're at each other's throats."

"Don't make this worse." She pulled her hand out of his grasp to hold his arm. "I'm begging you. Please, don't ruin everything we've worked for. It was such a long time ago. It's in the past. Don't tell him." Her chin trembled and her eyes started to shimmer.

Kirk had never seen his mother like this. All his life, she had been the most formidable force of nature he had ever known. No matter how paranoid she got, she was always in control. Always the one in charge. Now, she looked so small and fragile he sensed that she was on the verge of shattering. "What shouldn't Dad tell me?" he asked.

His father pulled his arm from his wife with a heavy sigh. "I know I talk a tough game, but I'm not going to lie to you right now, Kirk. Being in jail was a humbling experience. It's given me time to think about what I really want out of life. Especially when I realized that if these charges go to a trial, I could go to prison for a long time. So it's time, son. Time for me to confess the truth."

Chapter 15

K irk's insides knotted. He could feel the tension coiling in his stomach.

"No, Bruno, don't tell him," his mother cried out. "We promised we'd never talk about this to anyone."

"We also promised to protect our sons," his father muttered. "If we go to prison, we sure as hell won't be able to protect them from behind bars. With the truth, they'll be able to protect themselves."

Whatever this secret was, it was bad enough to make his mother completely fall apart.

The sinking feeling in the pit of his stomach intensified. Bethany had wondered if his parents had committed the crimes they were accused of. Like a fool he had thought that, even if they had, it couldn't be as bad as anything Lloyd Livingston had done. Now, he wasn't so sure anymore. "You can tell me, Dad," Kirk said.

"It involves Lloyd Livingston," his father said after a moment.

"It always involves him," Vivian wailed.

"Let me finish, Vivian." Blowing out a frustrated breath, his father put out his cigar in an ashtray on one of the low side tables. "This is about what happened before Livingston's first arrest ten years ago."

His heart hammered wildly, slamming against his chest as the enormity of the moment dawned on him. Sudden regret gave him pause. Bethany should be here for this. After all, it was about her father. The father who was languishing in jail. "What happened, Dad?"

"I know we've always been treated like heroes for revealing the truth about Lloyd's embezzlement," his father said. "The media hailed us as whistleblowers. We took over the bank from Lloyd, then discovered what he'd been doing all along and went to the authorities. Even though we had only just started to lead the bank, we took a huge risk by telling the world about Lloyd's embezzlement."

"You saved people from becoming his victims." His mouth went dry. The sinking sensation that his illusions were about to be shattered was overpowering.

"The truth is, Kirk, we knew about Lloyd's embezzlement long before we told the police," his father said.

Silence as loud as a jet engine filled the room. In this moment, Kirk would give anything to hold on to his illusions. To doubt that his parents could ever be capable of telling such a lie for so long. "You knew?"

His father nodded grimly. "We knew. For years."

"What? Why didn't you say anything?" Kirk paused to think, his mind racing a million miles a minute. "You were scared, weren't you? Back then you might have risen up the ranks at the Livingston Bank, but Lloyd was virtually all-powerful. You'd never dare go against him until you were powerful enough to do so."

"No. That's not it at all." His father gave him a hard, unflinching stare. "Don't try to cover for us. Don't try to make us look like victims here. Trust me, son, we're not the victims of this sorry affair."

"Okay. So, you knew about Lloyd's theft years before you told the police," Kirk murmured. "Why did you keep that kind of information to yourselves?"

"Because we planned on using the information to our advantage," his father said flatly. "We found out about the stolen money, and about other things going on at the bank. We decided to keep our mouths shut about all of it until the time was right. Your mother and I allowed Lloyd to keep on embezzling. All that time we knew and we could have spared all those innocent people a world of pain. One of Lloyd's victim's suicides... that victim lost all their money in the years after we knew."

"*Dammit.*" Something in him snapped. Broke in two. Earlier, he had said he didn't recognize his parents, but that was nothing compared to the turmoil raging inside Kirk now. Not recognizing them was one thing. Being ashamed of them was another thing entirely.

"We kept the truth to ourselves, using everything we learned about Lloyd's shady investments to game the system. The more we did, the more contacts we made. We amassed the board's support and quietly pushed out Lloyd's allies. Finally, when we used our new-found power to force Lloyd out, we knew it was time to strike." His father took a deep, shuddering breath. "Then we did strike. We went to the police. Not because we were heroes trying to do the right thing. But because we wanted to make sure Lloyd went to prison so that we could keep the bank under our control. Lloyd needed to go to prison if we had any hope of holding on to the financial empire we had taken from him."

For all these years he had kept on believing in his parents because they had reported Lloyd Livingston's crimes to the police. No matter how much his belief wavered, he had held on to that one heroic act. The act of people looking out for their clients and employees. The act of people who knew right from wrong no matter what other lines they crossed.

"The client who committed suicide..." His voice trailed off. Too afraid to know the depths his parents had sunk to in order to gain wealth and power.

"He had a family," his mother breathed. "Children who depended on him. Which is why your father and I took care of his family. Gave them the money they would need—"

"What good is that money if their father was dead?" Kirk balled up his hands in anguished fury. "Please, tell me you gave them that money out of some kindness. Tell me there's a shred of decency in you."

"We gave them money because we never wanted the truth to come back to us," his father said. "We figured that if we gave the poor man's family some money, it would make us look good and remove any doubt about our role in Livingston's crime."

"Your role in his crimes was that you knew all along and used it to get this." He gestured around the opulent living room in disgust. "A man died so that you could live like royalty."

"We did it to secure your future," his mother insisted. "I wasn't going to let my sons suffer through the same poverty I had to suffer through."

That future was quickly starting to slip away. His parents' arrest and the leak had been major setbacks for him professionally. All of that paled in comparison to the smoldering ruin of his personal life. Bethany had been attacked. And now, his parents had just confessed that the past ten years had been built on lies.

"Is that why you chose to let money launderers and other criminals do whatever they wanted at the bank?" he demanded in anger. "Is that why you decided to get Lloyd put in prison for a decade? Is that why you ruined Bethany's entire family? For me?"

"Yes," his mother answered in a small, pitiful voice.

"Now I understand the charges that were brought against you," he said in angry amazement. "The news had reported that you were all being charged with obstruction of justice and failure to report a crime. I had no idea that this is what you'd been hiding all this time. How the hell did the police even find out about this?"

Sighing, his father hung his head. "The money launderer I told you about probably told them. It looks like his last act before he skipped town was to make sure we got arrested. I don't know why he turned on us all of a sudden the way he did."

"Let me guess, the mysterious money launderer is Damien Kemp," he muttered.

Shock flashed in his father's eyes. "Yes, but how did you know that?"

"You kept your secrets for ten years, I think I'll keep mine," he said dryly. Kirk knew exactly why Damien Kemp had sent his police force after them. It had probably been the former police chief's revenge on him for taking so much of his money. He should have known that a vindictive man like Damien wouldn't stand to be humiliated. But telling his parents would only put Bethany in danger. There was no way in hell he would give his unscrupulous parents more ammo to use against her. Not now that he knew they were capable of anything to get whatever they wanted.

Bitter disappointment knifed through his stomach. For all these years he had believed in his parents. While he never thought they were perfect, he had believed that he had reason to be proud of them. Not anymore. His pride in them was now being replaced with contempt.

"So Damien Kemp knew that you had lied?" he asked.

"Yes," his father replied. "Kemp wanted us to take over the bank and enter into a secret partnership with him. We'd have control of the bank while he laundered all the money he needed for his bosses. Unfortunately for us, Damien figured out how we managed to get rid of Lloyd so he blackmailed us with it. Over time, he's been taking away more and more control away from us."

Kirk shot to his feet, too furious to spend another second in the mansion with his deceitful parents. "I can't listen to another second of this. To hell with both of you."

"You can't leave just yet," his father snarled.

He scowled at his dad. "Why the hell not?"

"We have the bank to save," Bruno said.

"A bank we own because of your lies," Kirk said harshly.

"A bank we will lose to Damien Kemp and his cronies," his father said. "Is that what you want?"

Tension made his body stiffen. There were now two opposing forces vying for his attention, and both choices compromised his integrity. If he helped his parents save SIB from ruin, he would be rewarding their lies and corruption. If he let it fall to teach them a lesson the bank would get into the wrong hands, and thousands of people could lose their jobs, life savings, or pensions.

Finally he said through clenched teeth, "No, I don't want Kemp getting control of the bank."

"Well, I've been brought up to speed about the leak and I'm guessing that's the other topic you wanted to talk about," his father said. "You want us to come up with a plan to save the bank, don't you?"

"Yes, that's what I wanted," he replied slowly.

"Fine. You can punish us later, after we've gotten SIB back on solid footing," his mother said. "Right now, we don't have time to squabble. You tell us everything you know about the leak, and we'll get you up to speed on the backroom deals we've made recently."

He balled up his hands again, bitter bile rising in his throat. "What about Bethany?"

His mom pursed her lips in disapproval. "Since your father has so foolishly explained what we're up against, I suppose we can go back to fighting the Livingstons after the bank is saved. You'll be able to have your fun with her for the next few weeks at least."

Helping the save the bank meant that he was literally helping his mother regain the power she would need to destroy Bethany. "I can't accept that," he said flatly. "If you want my help, you'll leave Bethany alone."

"Does that mean I have to accept her? Invite her to events? Treat her like one of the family?" his mother snapped. "Because I won't."

"All you have to do is leave her in peace," he said icily.

"Fine." The expression on his mother's face hardened. "Don't think for a moment that extends to the rest of her family."

Right now, it was the best he was going to get from his mother. He might regret agreeing to her terms in the future, but right now he needed to protect Bethany. Even if her family ended up paying for it.

He gave her a curt nod. "Fine. Though I can't imagine what more you could do for Lloyd. Not even his fancy lawyer could get him out of jail."

His father scoffed in response. "What fancy lawyer? Livingston has been stuck with a public defender."

Kirk frowned. "No, that's not right." He couldn't tell his parents that he had paid for Lloyd's new lawyer, so he'd have to fudge some of the details. "I heard Bethany talk to her brother about their father's attorney. Somehow her brother managed to raise the funds to get their dad a better lawyer."

"I saw Lloyd's lawyer come and go while I was in jail," his dad said with a shake of his head. "His lawyer was some public defender provided by the government. Christ, you should have seen the cheap suit he wore. It was the same damn suit every day. Plus, he looked like he was twelve years old. Fresh out of law school, that one."

An unfamiliar dread settled in his gut. He had given thousands of dollars to Bethany's brother to pay for a better lawyer. If Joshua hadn't hired a new lawyer for his father, where the hell had all that money gone?

Suddenly, an unsettling notion flashed in his mind. If Joshua hadn't paid for a better lawyer, that meant he wanted his father to stay in jail. Alarm bells went off in his head. Something wasn't adding up. Instinct told him that the conspiracy at the bank had just gotten bigger. All he needed to do was connect the dots.

The major problem was that he couldn't tell Bethany about her brother. With an embezzling father in jail again, having her brother turn out to be a crook as well would be a total shock. Telling her that her brother was a liar and a thief would break her heart even if he had a mountain of evidence. He'd need to get proof before he broke the news to her. News he only wanted to tell her to protect her. Not break her heart the way he knew it inevitably would.

Worst of all, he had come to his parents' mansion thinking that he had to protect Bethany from his family. Now he realized that, with Joshua's shady behavior, the family he'd have to protect her from was her own.

———◦———

TAKING THE TIME TO relax by the swimming pool had been a good idea, though she hated to admit it to herself. Bethany was stretched out on a chaise longue, enjoying the last rays of the setting sun. Once it got completely dark, she'd head into the mansion to make sure the chef had started dinner. She wanted Kirk to come home to a hot meal after dealing with his parents.

"There you are."

Kirk's deep baritone startled her for a moment, but she recovered quickly enough to give him a smile. "You're home. How did everything go?" She got up and walked over to him.

Her smile faded when she caught the grave expression on his face.

Even beneath the outside lights overhead, she saw how pale his face was. How drained he looked. He looked defeated. That was the only word that sprang to mind as she approached him.

"Is everything okay?" She wrapped her arms around his broad shoulders and stared into his eyes.

"No."

"Oh, crap. Your parents." Apprehension slowly wrapped itself around her heart. Made it beat faster with each passing second. "They're angry that we're together, aren't they?"

"That's not it," he said. "Though they aren't exactly thrilled we're together."

"So, they've accepted us?" she asked.

"Accept is a strong word. They've just agreed to stop coming after you," he said tightly. "Can't say the same for the rest of your family, though."

Worry overtook her and she bit her lip. "What is it, then?"

Without a word, Kirk reached for her hand and walked with her back into the mansion in silence. When he released her hand, he crossed the living room to the liquor cabinet on the far wall. Pulling out a bottle of what looked like brandy, he said, "I'm going to need a drink for this. How about you?"

"No thanks," she said, settling onto the sofa.

He poured himself a drink and took the seat opposite her. "How was your day?"

Caught off guard by the unexpected question, she blinked in surprise. "Good. I texted my brother about Dad, though he hasn't replied. I was thinking we could try another lawyer, you know?"

"Don't bother talking to your brother about a lawyer," he said sharply.

"What?" Her eyes widened. "Why not?"

"Because I want to handle it." He swirled the brandy in his glass and took a gulp of the golden liquid. "I've got a whole team of lawyers I can choose from to help your father get out of jail. Don't stress your brother out right now."

"Are you sure?" she asked, still uncertain. "If my dad finds out that you're the one paying for his new lawyer, he's going to be really angry."

"I'll handle everything through a third-party legal team," he assured her.

"Won't that cost more?"

"Let me help you, Bethany," he said.

There was something strained about his voice. As if the subject was a burden he was tired of dealing with.

Guilt gnawed at her. Obviously he resented having to pay to get her dad out of jail. Spending the day with his parents had probably reminded him of his loyalties and obligations to his family. She decided to drop the subject for now. When he was in a better head space, she'd tell him not to bother paying for her dad's lawyer if it was going to cause tension in his family. That was the last thing she wanted, and she refused to selfishly take advantage of his generosity any more. Somehow, she'd have to get her dad out of jail another way.

"Okay," she said. "What happened?"

"My parents told me something," he answered quietly. "Something about your father."

Kirk inhaled a deep breath before telling her about his visit with his parents. Shock mounted with each detail he told her. By the time he was finished, she was sitting in stunned silence with her mouth agape.

"They knew?" she finally asked.

"Yes," he said, nodding. "They knew what your father was doing long before they told anyone."

"And Damien Kemp used it to blackmail them." She shook her head in disbelief, then swallowed hard as another thought struck her. "If they knew, then that means my dad really was guilty."

"Not necessarily," he said. "There's still a chance he was set up. Especially now that we know Damien Kemp and his goons were up to something."

"Maybe." She sighed. "It's just that, you've just learned something really awful about your parents. I might learn something awful about my dad, too."

"I promise we'll get to the bottom of everything," he assured her. "At least now we know what my parents have been hiding all these years."

She tried to take solace in that. At least the Sterling half of the mystery had been solved now. Though there were still so many questions. "This must be really hard for you to deal with, Kirk. I'm so sorry."

"It's definitely a shock, but I don't think I have the time to focus on that right now," he said.

Even though he seemed to want to put his feelings aside, she guessed that he would be in turmoil over this for a long time. Knowing that, she resolved to be there for him no matter what. She had to show him that she would always be ready to listen to his troubles. "So, what did your parents say after they confessed?"

Kirk averted his gaze suddenly to look down at the glass in his hand. He lifted the glass, bringing it to his lips to finish the remainder of the brandy. "They talked about a plan to save the bank."

"Oh." She tilted her head, studying him. Her instincts told her there was more he wasn't telling her. Probably about his own feelings. As much as she wanted to listen to him, she also didn't want to push him. Not right now, while he was clearly still processing what he had just learned. "What plan did they come up with?"

He forced out a breath and rubbed his temples. "They're going to send in a lawyer to quietly look into the staff at SIB's cyber security department. And we're going to look through who has been buying shares with a fine-toothed comb. If Damien Kemp has been buying bank shares at reduced rates for his cronies, I want to know about it."

"So, that means the cyber security officer who handled our devices will be looked into right?"

"Yes. That's the most important part of the plan," Kirk explained. "We'll secretly dig up everything we can about Edward Pryce and then I'll question him. That way he won't have time to come up with any convenient lies."

"That's clever," she said. "I knew your parents would come up with something. I'm just sorry you had to learn something so painful in the process."

"It's hard to learn the truth about family." Sadness darkened his green eyes, and he stared at her for a lingering moment. As if he knew more about that lesson than he was letting on. It made her heart squeeze in sympathy for him.

Now that she knew Kirk's parents were as shady as she had suspected, part of her wanted to turn back time. Being right wasn't worth it if he was going to be in so much pain.

"What can I do to help in the meantime?" she asked.

"Once I've gotten your dad a more experienced lawyer, I think you should talk to them," he responded. "Tell them everything you remember about your dad's previous conviction. The failure to report a crime charge is serious, but the police really need to have their ducks in a row to make that stick. The real hurdle is the obstruction charge. Giving your dad's new lawyer details about how your dad did the right thing by taking a plea deal ten years ago might go a long way toward making the charges go away."

"That sounds like a solid plan," she said. "I'll let my brother know—"

"No, don't talk to Joshua about this," Kirk said quickly. "My parents think he's too emotional to handle this at the moment. Same with your mother. Best to limit contact with both of them for the time being. He could be reckless and compromise your father's case, which is the last thing we need."

She chewed her lip. Her brother had been reckless enough to try to raise bail from criminals. A dangerous decision like that could definitely put their dad in even more legal jeopardy. Bethany didn't like keeping her brother out of the loop, but if it saved their father then she was willing to make the sacrifice. "Okay. I'll talk to the lawyer, but I won't tell my brother or my mom."

He let out a sigh that sounded more like relief than anything else. Picking up his parents from jail had surely stressed him out. Desperate to soothe his obvious pain, she slid off the sofa and headed over to him.

Bethany sat down beside him, giving him an encouraging smile. "I'll always be here to listen to you."

"I know you will." He pressed his lips to the top of her head for a kiss. "You're why I'm the luckiest man in the world. If it weren't for you, I'd have no family left."

Heart aching for him, she tucked her legs under her and snuggled up against him. "We'll get through this. I know it doesn't look like it now, but one day our families will be whole again."

"I hope you're right, Bethany. I hope you're right."

Chapter 16

"You're going to tell me the truth." Kirk tossed a manila envelope onto his desk and glared at the cyber security officer sitting across from him.

Edward Pryce swallowed hard, squirming in his chair. "Mr. Sterling, what's this about?"

It had been a few weeks since his parents had sent lawyers to dig up dirt on the cyber security department. Kirk had only just gotten the results of that investigation this morning. If he wanted to catch the cyber security officer in a lie, it was best to do it right now. Before he came up with an escape plan and vanished the way Damien Kemp had.

"You haven't been loyal to the bank," Kirk said from his seat at his office desk. "I'm giving you this chance to come clean. You might not be able to save your job, but at least you won't end up in prison for what you've done."

"Prison?" Edward's face turned white. "Please, Mr. Sterling, I'm begging you. Don't call the cops on me. I was only doing what I was told."

Based on what the investigation had turned up, that much was true. Edward really was secretly working with someone to undermine the bank. And Kirk already knew who it was. He just wanted to hear the truth come out of Edward's mouth. "Who are you working for, Edward?"

"Sir, promise me you won't tell them that I spilled the beans," Edward begged. "Promise me you'll tell them you figured it out on your own. If they think I've betrayed them, they'll destroy me."

Kirk cracked his knuckles. "If you don't tell me what you've done, I'll do more than destroy you," he warned in a menacing tone. If he could have avoided threatening Edward he would have. But thousands of people's livelihoods were at stake, and so was Bethany's relationship with her family.

For these past couple of weeks she had kept her word and avoided contact with her brother. It had bought him time to gather enough evidence to convince her of Joshua's guilt. The truth was that her brother had lied about hiring a better lawyer for their dad. Instead of paying for a more experienced lawyer, Joshua had pocketed the money for himself. He had let his own father suffer in prison for financial gain. That truth would crush her spirit.

Now that Kirk had hired a new lawyer for her father, there was a better chance that her father would get out of jail. Then he wouldn't have an excuse to prevent her from contacting her brother. With time running out, he had to gather the last piece of evidence from Edward Pryce. One he got it, he'd be able to gently break the truth to Bethany without letting her deal with the shock of finding out from someone else.

Edward held up shaking hands. "Okay. Okay. I'll tell you the truth. Just don't call the police on me. Please. The police are on his side and they'll finish me."

"His side. You mean Damien Kemp?" Kirk asked.

Edward nodded. "Yes. He's one of the people who forced me to do this. Kemp knew about my prior arrests because of my hacking. He was the police chief, so he had access to my records. Kemp swore that if I didn't do what he said, he'd tell SIB management that I lied about having a clean police record. I was going to lose my job if I didn't do as he said."

That had been pretty close to Kirk's theory. A police chief would have a wealth of information to use against his enemies. And Damien Kemp had a lot of enemies. "So, I'm guessing Damien Kemp approached you."

"That's right," Edward confirmed, his eyes darting around nervous-ly. "Damien had already left town, but he called me. Threatened me about my prior records." He winced. "Since he was out of town he sent one of his associates to make sure I was doing as I was told."

"Who was the associate?" Kirk demanded, knowing full well who it was.

"Joshua Livingston," Edward said, his voice shaking. "Lloyd Liv-ingston's son. He's been working for Kemp for a long time. He's kind of like a right-hand man or something."

There it was. The confirmation he needed. Kirk raked a hand through his hair and blew out a breath. Bethany's brother had been working for Kemp and his money-laundering goons for a long time now. It would destroy her to know that her brother had been so ob-sessed with regaining the wealth the Livingstons had lost that he was willing to betray his own family to do it.

"So, what was their plan?" Kirk asked.

"They wanted me to get secret information that could ruin the bank," he said. "First Joshua got intel from your home office—"

"*What*?" That unexpected detail was like a punch in the gut. Kirk thought back to the day Joshua had showed up to his mansion. Though he hadn't seen Bethany's brother do anything shady, there had been sev-eral minutes that went by with Joshua unsupervised. Which meant that he'd had more than enough time to sneak into Kirk's home study and get confidential information about SIB. There had definitely been in-formation about SIB hiring a temporary bank president while his par-ents dealt with their legal woes.

That confidential information had been leaked to media, damaging the bank's reputation in the process. Even now, weeks later, they were still dealing with the fallout. Clients had already started taking their money out of the bank in droves.

"He found out that you wanted to hire a temporary bank presi-dent," Edward continued. "Once he passed that on to me, it was my job to get the names of the candidates for that job. So, I got access to your laptop and your phone. That's how I got the names."

"Then you leaked the intel to the press. That tanked SIB shares," Kirk said.

Edward nodded. "Right. After share prices started falling, Damien and his bosses bought them."

That was the one piece of the puzzle that Kirk hadn't been able to figure out. The investigation hadn't given him any clues either. "We've checked for unusual activity with shares. Tried to figure out if anyone has been buying more shares than usual, but we haven't been able to find anything."

"Damien definitely bought them," Edward said. "He's probably figured out a way to do it without it looking suspicious. I'm telling you, that guy is the smartest person I've ever had to deal with. He's always ten steps ahead."

"Let me guess, Damien was the one who got my parents arrested?"

"Yeah."

Kirk frowned. "Revenge meant that much to him?"

"It did, but it was more than revenge," Edward explained. "He wanted to distract you. Damien thought that if you were so focused on getting your parents out of jail you wouldn't be paying attention to the bank."

"Is that why he attacked my girlfriend?" Kirk demanded, unable to suppress his anger for another second. "He put her in the hospital."

Edward winced again. "Damien attacked her to get her laptop. He thought he'd be able to get his money back with it. When that didn't work, he came up with the plan to buy the bank shares."

"So, how does Lloyd Livingston fit into all this?" Kirk asked.

"According to Damien, Lloyd knows too much. He's a loose end that Damien has been trying to tie up," Edward said. "Plus, with Lloyd out of the way, that meant his son could do whatever he wanted without his dad looking over his shoulder. That's another reason Damien was so desperate to get his money back. He was supposed to keep paying off Joshua Livingston. When the money didn't materialize, Joshua saw a way to scam some money from his dad's arrest."

"By pretending to pay for a new lawyer for his father," Kirk added. "I figured. Joshua pretended to care about getting his dad out of jail just so he could get his hands on some cash. First by raising funds for his dad's bail. When he didn't make enough money doing that, he saw an opening with me. All he had to do was pretend to give a damn about getting his dad out, then he'd take all the money that had been meant for the lawyers."

"They're kind of a messed-up family," Edward said.

"I think both families are messed up," Kirk muttered. It was much tougher for him to judge now that he knew the truth about his own parents.

"Yeah, well, Joshua isn't just in it for the money," Edward said. "He hates his sister. Resents her for coming out of the family mess relatively unscathed. Everyone has paid for the family's ruin, except for her. That's why he leaked her location to the press. He wanted to make her life as bad as possible."

And to think, Bethany had believed her mother had been the one to leak her whereabouts to the press. Kirk stood up. "I need to go." If he didn't tell Bethany as soon as possible, he'd lose his nerve.

"Does this mean I'm free to go, Mr. Sterling?" Edward asked.

"For now." Kirk narrowed his eyes. "Just know that from now on I'll be watching you."

"I can't just stop working for Damien," Edward said. "He'll finish me. My career will be over and I'll end up in prison."

"You won't stop working for him," Kirk said. "You'll keep working for him, but you'll report everything he says to me. Is that clear?"

Sweat formed on Edward's brow. "Yes, sir. Crystal clear."

"Now go." Kirk folded his arms and watched Edward rush out of the office.

Too bad he couldn't run away from his problems that easily. Somehow he was going to have to finally tell Bethany that her family would probably always be broken.

<hr />

SHE HUNG UP THE PHONE, so elated that she almost started dancing in the living room. Joshua had just called her with the good news. Charges against their father had been dropped. He was going to be released from jail any day now.

Now was the perfect time for an impromptu celebration. It was probably a little over-indulgent, but she had the sudden urge to raid Kirk's wine cellar for his best Champagne. Deciding to do just that, she got up from the sofa and set aside her sketchbook.

Part of her routine over these past few weeks to unwind after a long day of negotiating with her dad's lawyer and making plans for her shop was to sketch design ideas.

Out of the corner of her eye, she spotted Kirk walk into the living room. Overcome with joy and excitement, she flung her arms around him and trailed kisses across his handsome face. "You're here. Kirk, you won't believe the good news. My dad is getting out of jail. The charges have been dropped."

Kirk didn't respond. In fact, his entire body had gone rigid. She pulled back from him in surprise. "What happened? Are your parents okay?"

He didn't meet her gaze. Instead, he reached for her hands and looked down. "I have to tell you something. I think you should sit down."

"No, I want to stand," she said firmly, even though her heart was racing. Cold dread slithered down her spine. "What is it?"

"I have to tell you something about your brother. He's perfectly safe, so don't go thinking the worst."

"Okay," she said before she took a deep breath to calm herself.

"Your brother's partially to blame for your father being in jail all this time." He held up a manila envelope that she was only now just noticing.

With shaking hands, she took the folder from him and started to pull out the documents inside.

She listened as Kirk explained everything he had learned earlier that day. He told her how her brother had been working with Damien all along. How he had snuck into Kirk's home study to get intel that Damien could use against the bank. How he had taken money meant to pay for a better lawyer for their dad. A better lawyer that their father hadn't gotten, which was why he was stuck with his court-appointed public defender. That was why his second attempt at making bail had failed. With an inexperienced lawyer, and a prior conviction, Lloyd had been climbing an uphill slope.

When Kirk told her that her own brother had been the one to leak her location to the media, tears spilled down her cheeks. Joshua knew full well how much the press frightened her after all those years of torment. Yet he had sent reporters after her anyway.

All the documents in the envelope confirmed everything Kirk had said. SIB's investigators had done a thorough job. There was no denying it. Joshua had betrayed them all.

"How could he do this?" Overcome with pain, she held on to him. "How could he be so cruel?"

Kirk wrapped his strong arms around her, whispering encouraging words to her. "What matters now is that your dad is getting out. If you can't have a relationship with your brother, maybe you'll get a chance to reconnect with your dad after all this time."

Her father. He was still getting out of jail. That was something to be happy about.

Bethany swiped at her tears. "You're right. There might be a chance for me and my dad to reconcile now."

The sound of the doorbell ringing made her freeze.

"Oh, no." Her pulse quickened, anxiety flooding her. "That's probably my brother. I completely forgot that Josh said he was coming over to celebrate our dad's release."

"That son of a bitch." Kirk pulled away from her to march across the living room, but she placed a hand on his shoulder to stop him.

"Let me deal with this," she said.

"I'm not letting you deal with him on your own," Kirk said firmly.

She nodded, grateful to have his support. "Just promise you won't hurt him."

"Fine. I promise."

They headed for the front door, only to find a maid opening it.

A young man wearing a bicycle helmet walked inside.

Bethany frowned, realizing that she didn't recognize the young man at all.

"Who are you?" Kirk asked.

The man pulled out a rolled-up paper from his back pocket and unrolled it. "Are you Kirk Sterling?" he asked, glancing down at the paper.

Kirk scowled. "Yes. Now answer the question. Who are you?"

"And you're Bethany Walker?" the man asked, ignoring Kirk.

"Yes," she replied, still confused.

"Congratulations, folks, you've been served." The young man shoved the document into her hand and rushed back out.

"What the hell?" Kirk took the paper out of her hands and looked down at it. His brow furrowed, his anger evident. "Oh, shit."

"Kirk? What does it say?"

Kirk looked up at her, his stare hard and unyielding. "It's a lawsuit. Filed by your father. He's suing us."

THE END

Treasured Forever Blurb

Love hath no fury like a woman scorned!

Find Lexy Timms:

LEXY TIMMS NEWSLETTER:
http://eepurl.com/9i0vD
Lexy Timms Facebook Page:
https://www.facebook.com/SavingForever
Lexy Timms Website:
http://www.lexytimms.com

Want

FREE READS?

Sign up for Lexy Timms' newsletter
And she'll send you updates on new releases,
ARC copies of books and a whole lotta fun!

Sign up for news and updates!

http://eepurl.com/9i0vD

More by Lexy Timms:

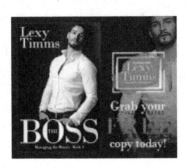

FROM BEST SELLING AUTHOR, Lexy Timms, comes a billionaire romance that'll make you swoon and fall in love all over again.

Jamie Connors has given up on men. Despite being smart, pretty, and just slightly overweight, she's a magnet for the kind of guys that don't stay around.

Her sister's wedding is at the foreground of the family's attention. Jamie would be fine with it if her sister wasn't pressuring her to lose weight so she'll fit in the maid of honor dress, her mother would get off her case and her ex-boyfriend wasn't about to become her brother-in-law.

Determined to step out on her own, she accepts a PA position from billionaire Alex Reid. The job includes an apartment on his property and gets her out of living in her parent's basement.

Jamie has to balance her life and somehow figure out how to manage her billionaire boss, without falling in love with him.

** The Boss is book 1 in the Managing the Bosses series. All your questions won't be answered in the first book. It may end on a cliff hanger.

For mature audiences only. There are adult situations, but this is a love story, NOT erotica.

FRAGILE TOUCH

"HIS BODY IS PERFECT. He's got this face that isn't just heart-melting but actually kind of exotic..."

Lillian Warren's life is just how she's designed it. She has a high-paying job working with celebrities and the elite, teaching them how to better organize their lives. She's on her own, the days quiet, but she likes it that way. Especially since she's still figuring out how to live with her recent diagnosis of Crohn's disease. Her cats keep her company, and she's not the least bit lonely.

Fun-loving personal trainer, Cayden, thinks his neighbor is a killjoy. He's only seen her a few times, and the woman looks like she needs a drink or three. He knows how to party and decides to invite her to over—if he can find her. What better way to impress her than take care of her overgrown yard? She proceeds to thank him by throwing up in his painstakingly-trimmed-to-perfection bushes.

Something about the fragile, mysterious woman captivates him.

Something about this rough-on-the-outside bear of a man attracts Lily, despite her heart warning her to tread carefully.

Faking It Description:

HE GROANED. THIS WAS torture. Being trapped in a room with a beautiful woman was just about every man's fantasy, but he had to remember that this was just pretend.

Allyson Smith has crushed on her boss for years, but never dared to make a move. When she finds herself without a date to her brother's upcoming wedding, Allyson tells her family one innocent white lie: that she's been dating her boss. Unfortunately, her boss discovers her lie, and insists on posing as her boyfriend to escort her to the wedding.

Playboy billionaire Dane Prescott always has a new heiress on his arm, but he can't get his assistant Allyson out of his head. He's fought his attraction to her, until he gets caught up in her scheme of a fake relationship.

One passionate weekend with the boss has Allyson Smith questioning everything she believes in. Falling for a wealthy playboy like Dane is against the rules, but if she's just faking it what's the harm?

Capturing Her Beauty

KAYLA REID HAS ALWAYS been into fashion and everything to do with it. Growing up wasn't easy for her. A bigger girl trying to squeeze into the fashion world is like trying to suck an entire gelatin mold through a straw; possible, but difficult.

She found herself an open door as a designer and jumped right in. Her designs always made the models smile. The colors, the fabrics, the styles. Never once did she dream of being on the other side of the lens. She got to watch her clothing strut around on others and that was good enough.

But who says you can't have a little fun when you're off the clock?

Sometimes trying on the latest fashions is just as good as making them. Kayla's hours in front of the mirror were a guilty pleasure.

A chance meeting with one of the company photographers may turn into more than just an impromptu photo shoot.

Hot n' Handsome, Rich & Single... how far are you willing to go?
MEET ALEX REID, CEO of Reid Enterprise. Billionaire extra ordinaire, chiseled to perfection, panty-melter and currently single.

Learn about Alex Reid before he began Managing the Bosses. Alex Reid sits down for an interview with R&S.

His life style is like his handsome looks: hard, fast, breath-taking and out to play ball. He's risky, charming and determined.

How close to the edge is Alex willing to go? Will he stop at nothing to get what he wants?

Alex Reid is book 1 in the R&S Rich and Single Series. Fall in love with these hot and steamy men; all single, successful, and searching for love.

Book One is FREE!
SOMETIMES THE HEART needs a different kind of saving... find out if Charity Thompson will find a way of saving forever in this hospital setting Best-Selling Romance by Lexy Timms

Charity Thompson wants to save the world, one hospital at a time. Instead of finishing med school to become a doctor, she chooses a different path and raises money for hospitals – new wings, equipment, whatever they need. Except there is one hospital she would be happy to never set foot in again—her fathers. So of course, he hires her to create a gala for his sixty-fifth birthday. Charity can't say no. Now she is working in the one place she doesn't want to be. Except she's attracted to Dr. Elijah Bennet, the handsome playboy chief.

Will she ever prove to her father that's she's more than a med school dropout? Or will her attraction to Elijah keep her from repairing the one thing she desperately wants to fix?

HEART OF THE BATTLE Series

In a world plagued with darkness, she would be his salvation.

No one gave Erik a choice as to whether he would fight or not. Duty to the crown belonged to him, his father's legacy remaining beyond the grave.

Taken by the beauty of the countryside surrounding her, Linzi would do anything to protect her father's land. Britain is under attack and Scotland is next. At a time she should be focused on suitors, the men of her country have gone to war and she's left to stand alone.

Love will become available, but will passion at the touch of the enemy unravel her strong hold first?

THE RECRUITING TRIP

Aspiring college athlete Aileen Nessa is finding the recruiting process beyond daunting. Being ranked #10 in the world for the 100m hurdles at the age of eighteen is not a fluke, even though she believes that one race, where everything clinked magically together, might be. American universities don't seem to think so. Letters are pouring in from all over the country.

As she faces the challenge of differentiating between a college's genuine commitment to her or just empty promises from talent-seeking coaches, Aileen heads to the University of Gatica, a Division One school, on a recruiting trip. Her best friend dares who to go just to see the cute guys on the school's brochure.

The university's athletic program boasts one of the top hurdlers in the country. Tyler Jensen is the school's NCAA champion in the hurdles and Jim Thorpe recipient for top defensive back in football. His incredible blue-green eyes, confident smile and rock hard six pack abs mess with Aileen's concentration.

His offer to take her under his wing, should she choose to come to Gatica, is a temping proposition that has her wondering if she might be with an angel or making a deal with the devil himself.

THE ONE YOU CAN'T FORGET

Emily Rose Dougherty is a good Catholic girl from mythical Walkerville, CT. She had somehow managed to get herself into a heap trouble with the law, all because an ex-boyfriend has decided to make things difficult.

Luke "Spade" Wade owns a Motorcycle repair shop and is the Road Captain for Hades' Spawn MC. He's shocked when he reads in the paper that his old high school flame has been arrested. She's always been the one he couldn't forget.

Will destiny let them find each other again? Or what happens in the past, best left for the history books?

** This is book 1 of the Hades' Spawn MC Series. All your questions may not be answered in the first book.

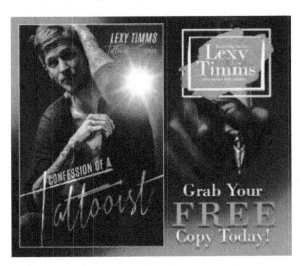

Don't miss out!

Visit the website below and you can sign up to receive emails whenever Lexy Timms publishes a new book. There's no charge and no obligation.

https://books2read.com/r/B-A-NNL-KDGV

BOOKS 2 READ

Connecting independent readers to independent writers.

Did you love *Knowing Your Worth*? Then you should read *Just Me* by Lexy Timms!

We all need somewhere where we feel safe...After leaving her abusive husband, Katherine Marshall is out on her own for the first time. She's hopped from city to city to avoid the man who made her life a living hell. When it seems she's finally found a new place where she begins to feel safe, she slowly grows confident that her life is looking up. A chance meeting with Ben O'Leary sets her life on a course and her soul on fire.Ben launched a business that went on to viral success while he was in college, and now as a thriving entrepreneur, he's most interested in maximizing profits. A billionaire living the dream But all that changes when he sets his eyes on Katherine. Things between the two heat up as they fall hard and fast—that is, until she gets an unexpected surprise that will test the strength of their relationship.You & Me - A Bad Boy RomanceBook 1 – Just MeBook 2 – Touch MeBook 3 – Kiss Me

Read more at www.lexytimms.com.

Also by Lexy Timms

A Burning Love Series
Spark of Passion

A Chance at Forever Series
Forever Perfect
Forever Desired
Forever Together

BBW Romance Series
Capturing Her Beauty
Pursuing Her Dreams
Tracing Her Curves

Beating the Biker Series
Making Her His
Making the Break
Making of Them

Billionaire Banker Series
Banking on Him
Price of Passion
Investing in Love
Knowing Your Worth

Billionaire Holiday Romance Series
Driving Home for Christmas
The Valentine Getaway
Cruising Love

Billionaire in Disguise Series
Facade
Illusion
Charade

Billionaire Secrets Series
The Secret
Freedom
Courage
Trust
Impulse
Billionaire Secrets Box Set Books #1-3

Building Billions
Building Billions - Part 1
Building Billions - Part 2
Building Billions - Part 3

Conquering Warrior Series
Ruthless

Diamond in the Rough Anthology
Billionaire Rock
Billionaire Rock - part 2

Dominating PA Series
Her Personal Assistant - Part 1
Her Personal Assistant Box Set

Fake Billionaire Series
Faking It
Temporary CEO
Caught in the Act
Never Tell A Lie
Fake Christmas

Firehouse Romance Series
Caught in Flames
Burning With Desire
Craving the Heat
Firehouse Romance Complete Collection

For His Pleasure
Elizabeth
Georgia
Madison

Fortune Riders MC Series
Billionaire Biker
Billionaire Ransom
Billionaire Misery

Fragile Series
Fragile Touch
Fragile Kiss
Fragile Love

Hades' Spawn Motorcycle Club
One You Can't Forget
One That Got Away

One That Came Back
One You Never Leave
One Christmas Night
Hades' Spawn MC Complete Series

Hard Rocked Series
Rhyme
Harmony
Lyrics

Heart of Stone Series
The Protector
The Guardian
The Warrior

Heart of the Battle Series
Celtic Viking
Celtic Rune
Celtic Mann
Heart of the Battle Series Box Set

Heistdom Series
Master Thief
Goldmine
Diamond Heist
Smile For Me

Just About Series
About Love
About Truth
About Forever

Justice Series
Seeking Justice
Finding Justice
Chasing Justice
Pursuing Justice
Justice - Complete Series

Love You Series
Love Life
Need Love
My Love

Managing the Bosses Series
The Boss
The Boss Too
Who's the Boss Now
Love the Boss
I Do the Boss
Wife to the Boss
Employed by the Boss
Brother to the Boss

Senior Advisor to the Boss
Forever the Boss
Christmas With the Boss
Billionaire in Control
Gift for the Boss - Novella 3.5
Managing the Bosses Box Set #1-3

Model Mayhem Series
Shameless
Modesty
Imperfection

Moment in Time
Highlander's Bride
Victorian Bride
Modern Day Bride
A Royal Bride
Forever the Bride

Outside the Octagon
Submit

Protecting Diana Series
Her Bodyguard
Her Defender
Her Champion

Her Protector
Her Forever

Protecting Layla Series
His Mission
His Objective
His Devotion

Racing Hearts Series
Rush
Pace
Fast

Reverse Harem Series
Primals
Archaic
Unitary

RIP Series
Track the Ripper
Hunt the Ripper
Pursue the Ripper

R&S Rich and Single Series

Alex Reid
Parker

Saving Forever
Saving Forever - Part 1
Saving Forever - Part 2
Saving Forever - Part 3
Saving Forever - Part 4
Saving Forever - Part 5
Saving Forever - Part 6
Saving Forever Part 7
Saving Forever - Part 8
Saving Forever Boxset Books #1-3

Shifting Desires Series
Jungle Heat
Jungle Fever
Jungle Blaze

Southern Romance Series
Little Love Affair
Siege of the Heart
Freedom Forever
Soldier's Fortune

Tattooist Series

Confession of a Tattooist
Surrender of a Tattooist
Heart of a Tattooist
Hopes & Dreams of a Tattooist

Tennessee Romance
Whisky Lullaby
Whisky Melody
Whisky Harmony

The Bad Boy Alpha Club
Battle Lines - Part 1
Battle Lines

The Brush Of Love Series
Every Night
Every Day
Every Time
Every Way
Every Touch

The Debt
The Debt: Part 1 - Damn Horse
The Debt: Complete Collection

Unlucky Series
Unlucky in Love
UnWanted
UnLoved Forever

Wet & Wild Series
Stormy Love
Savage Love
Secure Love

Worth It Series
Worth Billions
Worth Every Cent
Worth More Than Money

You & Me - A Bad Boy Romance
Just Me
Touch Me
Kiss Me

Standalone
Wash
Loving Charity
Summer Lovin'

Love & College
Billionaire Heart
First Love
Frisky and Fun Romance Box Collection
Beating Hades' Bikers

Watch for more at www.lexytimms.com.

About the Author

"Love should be something that lasts forever, not is lost forever."

Visit USA TODAY BESTSELLING AUTHOR, LEXY TIMMS
https://www.facebook.com/SavingForever

Please feel free to connect with me and share your comments. I love connecting with my readers.

Sign up for news and updates and freebies - I like spoiling my readers!

http://eepurl.com/9i0vD

website: www.lexytimms.com

Dealing in Antique Jewelry and hanging out with her awesome hubby and three kids, Lexy Timms loves writing in her free time.

MANAGING THE BOSSES is a bestselling 10-part series dipping into the lives of Alex Reid and Jamie Connors. Can a secretary really fall for her billionaire boss?

Read more at www.lexytimms.com.

Made in the USA
Coppell, TX
26 December 2020